The Longest Bloom

Copyright © 2025 Rashan Solun

ISBN: 978-1-63304-0717
Ebook: 978-1-63304-0724

First Printing: 2025

Editing: Raven's Eye
Formatting: Anne Battis
Cover Design: Michelle Brodeur

Portland, Oregon

The Longest Bloom

Rashah Solun

www.launchpointpress.com

About The Longest Bloom

Juliet is no stranger to death or grief—it's inevitable and comes with the territory of aging. But when she stands in front of her new bedroom mirror on her seventy-fifth birthday and sees the entirety of her naked body for the first time in a very long time, she is reminded that although the ghosts of her past at times haunt her, she is not yet a part of their world. So she vows to seek an awakening plan that will push her to live her life to the fullest. On this journey, she delves into her sexuality, searches for a long-lost love named Ruby, takes on the lessons of grief, loneliness, and the ups and downs that come with aging in a society that ignores older women of color, all while learning how to be at peace with the one person she can't escape—herself.

Author Notes

I wrote the first chapter for The Longest Bloom in April of 2020 in response to a senior paper for a class. The class was taught by Dr. Gloria Wade-Gayles at Spelman College and focused on oral history through the lens of age. I spent a year interviewing, documenting, and studying older Black women, their place in society, and their stories. My final paper focused on older Black women and their sexuality. I was surprised by how difficult it was to find studies on this topic. Although, after a year of seeing just how invisible older individuals are made to feel in our society, I shouldn't have been. Finding research information on older Black women, older women of color, and older queer women was nearly impossible. I knew their stories were out there. I knew older Black women weren't simply the asexual undesirable mammy figures that has been portrayed for generations throughout the media. In response to my need to see that these stories exist in the world, I decided to write my own.

I proceeded to write the first chapter right before graduation and didn't look at the story again for almost two years. Throughout those two years I wrote many manuscripts, but in all of my quiet moments I would hear the whisper of Juliet encouraging me to finish her story. Eventually that sweet encouragement became a fierce demand, so I set aside my other manuscripts and focused on Juliet's story. And I have to say I'm so glad I did. It is an honor to bring to the world a story about an older Black woman rediscovering the joys of life, love, and her sexuality while finding peace within herself.

Dedication

To the wild women whose wide hips I descended.
Thank you for showing me how to age with kindness and
spunk.

Acknowledgments

My heart is bursting with gratitude!

I must first thank Spirit for allowing me to be a vessel for every story waiting to be told.

Thank you to my son, Nullah, for being the embodiment of love and joy, and for reminding me every day to rejoice in the tiny moments of life. You're the reason I continue to write.

Thank you to my husband, Denzel, for being there when this story was a simple seed. Thank you for helping me water it along the way, for reading my first drafts, and for your reminders of perseverance that kept me afloat many days.

Thank you to my parents, Deborah and Jimmy Neason, for allowing my artist spirit to blossom during all of those years of dance rehearsals, piano practices, theatrical performances, and whatever else my curious heart desired to embark on.

Thank you to all the women in my Motherline, Deborah, Nellie, Juliet (no relation to the protagonist Juliet), and so on. I'm proud to be your continuation and to stand upon your shoulders.

Thank you to my older brothers, Jamal and Jahmad, and to the rest of my family for witnessing my journey.

Thank you to my literary agent, Najla Mamou, who saw something in my story and dared to take a risk on an up-and-coming writer.

Thank you to all of those at Launch Point Press for your commitment to sharing stories by and about queer folks/women, and for also seeing something worth sharing in Juliet's story.

And lastly, thank you to my former professor Dr. Gloria Wade-Gayles. If it weren't for your class, this story would not exist. You opened my eyes to see the rich lives older Black women are living. Thank you for reminding me to see the unseen, hear the unheard, and remember the forgotten.

Pendulum

I have swung to the uttermost reaches of pain,
'Mid the echo of sighs, and a deluge of rain,
But ah! I rebound to the limits of bliss,
On the rapturous swing of an infinite kiss.
*- **Georgia Douglas Johnson***

Chapter One

I HAVEN'T SEEN THE entirety of my naked body in a mirror since I was thirty-five. My body is a living memory of every breath I've taken for the last seventy-five years. Laugh lines and loose skin tell the story of a life before a husband, a child, bills to pay, mouths to feed, and more people exiting my life than I could've imagined. The azure-blue nightgown surrounds my feet like a pool of water. No one initiates you into aging. No one prepares you for death or life. Most days it feels like I'm drowning. But the mirror doesn't reflect a drowning woman. This woman can walk on water.

"I remember you."

The soft morning light acts as a spotlight from the heavens. Birds, who rose hours ago, share an especially loud song through the open window by my bed. The house shakes a bit when the occasional airplane passes overhead. It's a typical Sunday morning, except for me stripping off my cotton nightgown and standing in front of the full-length mirror behind my bedroom door. Perhaps it's a mix of sunlight and heat, unusual for Ohio's August and causing beads of sweat to slide down my spine, that makes me want to be naked. It's the type of heat that reminds me of growing up in South Georgia, the sticky kind that would soak through my Sunday dress while causing my freshly straightened hair to curl around the edges.

In my childhood home, I didn't have a full-length mirror. My mother, Claudine, always said, "From our shoulders up is for us. Everything below is for them." It took me years to understand what "them" meant but only seconds to internalize her words. She was a very religious woman who believed the devil personally invented vanity. For a while, like many indoctrinated children, so did I. Without question, I accepted the fact that I wasn't supposed to see my entire bare body in the mirror. I accepted that I would have to stay home and take care of my sick mother instead of going off to college. When it was time for me to get married, I accepted the proposal, and when it was time for me to have a child, I accepted my new role as a mother. Acceptance from everyone but myself saturated my life. I was comfortable drifting down a river following a current that was not my own.

Today is my birthday. Seventy-four came and went like all the other years. I no longer have anyone to care for; I'm no longer a wife. My years of mothering underneath my roof are long gone. I woke up hot and alone in bed. There's no longer a "them" in my life to see below my shoulders. Only me. My husband of fifty-one years, Roy, died four years ago, and getting out of bed every day began to feel like an obligation. Living became the antithesis of grieving. Time. Time is what everyone says will heal me. I went to group counseling and paid for therapists. I even stepped into a church on one occasion after I convinced myself I was being punished for not attending in years. I walked out knowing I would never return. Self-help books began to take over my art studio, and I was one of the vulnerable souls who fell for anything the experts and gurus tried selling me. But time didn't heal. The passage of years only allowed my mind to trick itself into believing Roy's death never happened. I could fool myself with distractions by spending time with my daughter or grandchildren. But after losing my best friend, I had lost myself.

Looking at my reflection, the dark-brown skin relaxing on my body, the short, curly grey hair sticking to my face from sweat, and the breast I once held my daughter under that gravity has befriended, tears roll down my soft cheeks. I'm not sad or angry about how I look. I'm sad and angry about how long it took me to look again. I've been to many funerals at this point in my life. I've seen my fair share of the lifeless bodies of loved ones and friends. And although on many occasions I've felt dead on the inside, the mirror confirms I'm still alive.

"You had the answers," I whisper to my reflection. With its slight tremor and protruding veins, I move my right hand over my navel and pouch that grew with time down to the grey coiled hairs between my thighs. As my hand continues to explore my body, Roy appears behind me, sitting on our bed.

"You sure lookin' good there, Mrs. Juliet. I think I'm gonna have to take you on a date."

"Oh yeah, and where are we gonna go?" I ask while wiping tears from my face.

"Well, I know you've always liked to eat, so I would take you to your favorite café for breakfast."

"And, what else?"

"You always loved to get out of the house on your birthday, so I would take you out dancing."

"You think you know me, old man?"

"I do indeed. I know you so well that before we even go out dancing, I would take you to that little hole-in-the-wall movie theater you always loved, just so we could watch some movie we'd have to read."

"You mean just so I could watch the movie, and you could fall asleep." I walk to sit next to him, his belly moving in and out from his deep, raspy laughter. I stare at the two of us in the mirror, and instead of breaking down into one of my many crying fits, I laugh with him.

"It's time for me to start living again, Roy."

"I agree."

"I used to be fun. Remember how fun I used to be?"

"Wild may be a better term," Roy says playfully.

"Now I look in the mirror, and I don't even know who that woman is."

"Why don't you find out?"

"You're right. I'm gonna find out, and I'm gonna make a plan. I'm no stranger to death. I know how it eats, sleeps, and breathes. I can easily die tomorrow, a year from now, or twenty years from now, and you know what I would feel? Regret. Regret for wasting the time I was given."

"What type of plan are you talking about, Peach?"

I smile after hearing Roy call me the nickname he's had for me since we met. He always said that his favorite fruit was peaches. When we met, his two favorite things about me were my face and my butt, and both reminded him of the shape of a peach. At first, I hated the name. I thought it meant that I looked round and needed to lose weight. Eventually, Peach grew on me.

"It'll be a plan for how I want to die. An awakening plan really," I say matter-of-factly.

Roy shakes his head back and forth with his lips pursed together.

"I don't think I like the sound of that plan. You're not thinkin' of ki—"

"Of course not! If I wanted to do that, I would've done it a long time ago. Believe me, it's not like the thought has never crossed my mind."

"Then what is this death plan of yours? It sounds crazy." His voice is stern. He's still looking out for me.

I get up from the bed, grab a small, yellow notebook from my nightstand, and pace around the room with the top of the pen in my mouth.

"Maybe, but it feels right. And it's not really about death. I mean I don't know how exactly I'm going to die, or when, or where, but I do know I'm tired of thinking about it all the time. I don't care. I do know how I want to live, and it's not like this."

I sit back down on the bed next to Roy and stare once more at my reflection in the mirror. The top of my back is slightly curved, and my skin is loose underneath my arms. My body is soft like the petals of a rose.

"Look at me." I study the shape of my body and how the brown rolls and wrinkles weave in and out of each other, becoming one. Roy smiles his gapped-tooth smile.

"It's like looking at a painting."

The sound of my cell phone pulls my eyes away from my reflection, and Roy disappears back into my subconscious. I give myself one last look and saunter over to my bed as if a lover is watching me. For a second, I allow for a version of myself to creep back into my body. She could stop traffic with her legs alone. I miss her.

There's a call from my daughter, Toni. Sweet girl, always concerned about the well-being of her mother. I call her back, and of course she answers on the first ring.

"Hello Mom, are you okay?"

"Yes baby, I'm okay."

"Just checking, you usually pick up on the first ring."

"Well, I was a little busy this morning."

"Doing what?"

"Minding mine."

"Okay, okay. Happy birthday, by the way! I thought we could have dinner. I know you didn't want to do anything this year, but I found this amazing caterer that I think you'll love. And I know you don't like cake but wait until you taste this one..." I allow Toni to continue talking, as I return to admiring myself in the mirror. Toni is so much like her father, organized and always wanting others to be happy. Sometimes Toni's happiness only comes from making others happy. This trait she got from me. It was only when I watched Toni grow into a woman and start a family of her own that I understood what false happiness and self-sacrifice looked like.

"Mom?"

"Yes, baby?"

"Did you hear what I said?"

"No, I got distracted. What were you saying?"

"I asked what time you want us to pick you up?"

"You know what, it's such a nice day outside. I think I'm gonna go for a walk and see where life takes me. Maybe I'll go to the movies too."

"And who's going with you?"

"As of right now, no one."

"So no dinner?"

"No dinner."

"No cake?"

"No Toni, no cake."

"You do know your grandchildren want to see you for your birthday…"

"Be sure to give them a kiss for me."

I know she's about to have a fit and try to take on the role of my mother, so I do what any reasonable mother with overgrown children would do. I hang up the phone. Looking down at my brittle, bare nails, I can't remember the last time I thought about painting them. Seems to be a pattern with me lately, not remembering the last I did something just for me, just for the pleasure of doing it. I convinced myself for years that there was no need to paint my nails when there was no one to paint them for. The bareness of my nails has a striking resemblance to my life. Plain, neglected, boring. That's it. I'm painting them. For me. But before I can finish my search for a bottle of nail polish, my granddaughter calls.

"Hello, Destiny."

"Hey Grandma, happy birthday!"

"Why thank you, sweetie."

"I'm sure you know I just got off the phone with Toni the Terror."

"Yeah, I figured." I pull a bottle of red nail polish from underneath my bed, which has probably been there for years.

With a few drops of nail polish remover and a quick shake, the red goo thins out just enough for me to meticulously paint each fingernail. I'll have to remember to pick up a new bottle when I go out.

"She said you're taking yourself out on a date."

"You know, I didn't look at it that way, but I guess I could call it a date."

"That's great, Grandma! I hope you have fun and enjoy your day. I'll try to calm Mom down as best as I can. Anyway, love ya, enjoy seventy-five, bye."

"I will. Love you too, bye."

After my nails dry, I walk to my closet and grab the brightest dress I can find, a yellow linen kaftan.

"This will do."

I slip into my dress and stare down at my vanity table. Each bottle of cream or oil I pick up has a label claiming its ability to stop my body from aging.

"It's no wonder I'm always trying to avoid the mirror." I smile at the pile of anti-aging cosmetics in my trash and slap on some lipstick, then call one of my closest friends.

"Well speaking of my much older friend Juliet, I was just thinking about the birthday lady. Happy birthday!"

"Thank you, Lili. Don't worry, you'll be joining me in the seventy-five club very soon."

"I still have a few months on my side, thank you. How are you spending your day? I'm sure Toni has a very detailed itinerary."

"She did, but I canceled."

"She's probably shittin' bricks."

"Probably, but I'm not in the mood for Toni's manicured birthday plans. Instead, we're going to go out for lunch."

"Well I can't say no can I, since it's your birthday and all? Even if it weren't, I would still come. I'm bored out of my mind."

"Good. Meet me at Café Daisy at one."

"See you then."

***

I feel strange sitting in this café by myself wearing this yellow dress like a little girl going to church on Easter. The last time I wore bright colors I was in my forties. I do like them. I'm an artist and color fills my world, yet I allowed my wardrobe to become as dull and predictable as my life.

Finally, Lili shows up almost twenty minutes late.

"I haven't been in this café in forever!" Lili walks over to my table like a whirlwind in her leather boots, skinny jeans, and oversized sunglasses. She's a proud Puerto Rican mother of five and grandmother of ten and counting. She tosses her wavy, black-and-silver hair over her shoulder and sits down.

"This place has really changed." Lili takes her sunglasses off and looks around.

"That it has. Remember when they had only one pot of black coffee."

"I surely do. And it cost only forty cents."

"I miss those prices, but I have to admit I do love that lavender syrup and goat's milk in my latte."

Lili laughs. "I bet you do. You were always a little bourgie Ms. World Traveler who partied at all the lavish artsy affairs."

"Says the woman in the eight-hundred-dollar boots."

Lili sits back in her seat and calls a waiter over. "Touché. Now why are we here, Juliet?"

I take a sip of my latte. "What do you mean? We're having lunch."

"Yes I know, but you don't have lunch. You rarely leave your house anymore. Now we talk all the time on the phone, but whenever I invite you out, you always turn me down. Why today?"

She always knew how to read me like a book. And she was never afraid to get straight to the point.

"Okay, you're right. I've been a hermit for years. But I'm tired of living like a monk. I'm not even a good monk. It's not like I've learned anything profound. I need to be back in the world, and I can't think of anyone better to start off this chapter with than you."

Lili reaches over and squeezes my hand. "It's about damn time! I always lived vicariously through you when you were off giving lectures in this country or that. When you stopped going out, I had no one to live through."

I smirk. "Well, I am so sorry you had to go through that. It must've been really tough for you."

"You should be and it was. Do you know how boring it was to listen to yet another person describe how fun their grandkid's birthday party was?"

"I enjoy my grandkids birthday parties."

"Sure you do. But I bet they don't compare to dancing under the stars somewhere in Casablanca with a glass of champagne in your hand."

"We'll just have to go on a girl's trip one day to make up for it."

"I'm holding you to that. But for now you must come to my spade's night on Saturday."

My first instinct is to say no. Saturdays are for reading in my pajamas and ordering Indian food. And Lili's spade's night has always been notoriously wild, especially when we were younger. Drinks, dancing, occasionally some reefer, and an all-nighter of playing spades. After Lili and Barnard divorced, spade's night became a ladies-only affair, which means that a bunch of women spend the evening talking very recklessly. But it's a part of my plan to be more adventurous and spend more time with friends. I make a mental note to get a lot of rest the night before.

"Fine. I'll be there."

"I envy you, Juliet. You're taking the steps that most of us never take. We stick to our ways until it's time for us to go."

"Well, I've got a long way to go. I might've said fine, but I still have to show up."

We both laugh and order salads. I add a tuna sandwich. The hours go by without us realizing, until Lili is called away to babysit one of her granddaughters.

"See you Saturday!"

She waves from her car as she drives off. I look around at my ever-changing town in Maplehorn, Ohio. The mom-and-pop stores are now a Starbucks and a soon-to-be Trader Joe's. Fathers in shorts that barely reach their thighs are running while pushing their babies in strollers. More people than I can count walk past, talking on their cell phones or listening to music. And dogs of all shapes and sizes are being walked, pushed in strollers, or carried. What an interesting time we live in. I remember when only mothers walked their babies on this street and dogs were only walked on leashes.

My steps are light, as I walk to the hole-in-the-wall movie theater up the street. The sun is peaking in and out of the clouds, and people aren't crowding the sidewalks. I'm able to walk at my own pace without feeling the eyes of someone behind me wishing I would move faster. It's a typical Sunday afternoon, humid but bearable. The theater is practically empty, which isn't surprising. There aren't a lot of people who prefer to spend their Sunday afternoons watching an indie film as opposed to a football game. I used to drag Roy here almost every week, back when they had penny movies, and eventually dollar movies. I would get lost in the film, while Roy became lost in his dreams.

I settle into my seat with a box of chocolate-covered raisins and wonder what I'm watching. I can't even remember the title of the film from when I bought the ticket five minutes ago. There are four other people in the theater with me. The couple in front of me starts kissing before the lights have dimmed. A man behind me sits with a notebook in his hand, and an employee is stretched out across the seats in a corner, snoring softly. I check my phone. It's been twenty minutes. The film is set in Italy and follows two young women, around Destiny's age, who are falling in love with one another. The beginning was very, very slow, but now I'm leaning closer and closer to the screen with every passing minute. I'm fully engrossed in the young love before me, so pure and innocent. Can anyone else hear my heartbeat? Or my thoughts? Thoughts of a secret love I once had and made myself forget a long time ago. That love was also young and pure, a love named Ruby.

Chapter Two

I HAVEN'T GONE OUT in town by myself in years. I've missed it. I miss me. I miss laughing and gossiping with Lili about the new neighbor she had a secret crush on. I miss getting dolled up, doing my hair, picking out an outfit, and putting on a little lipstick. The sun and air felt different on my skin today, freer. Day one of this journey was more than I could've imagined. I thought I would simply take myself out on a date. I thought I would experience what it feels like to be content with being with just me. I never imagined I would think of Ruby again. Is it even worth my time to imagine the life she's living, has lived? Or to daydream about the life we once lived together? I don't want to waste any more time wallowing than I already have. Am I kidding myself to dig up memories of someone buried deeply in my heart?

***

I've been tossing and turning all night. I want to throw a shoe at the fan in the corner of the room for failing to cool down my body and thoughts. I try reading, watching television, painting, and drinking chamomile tea. The book is boring after three lines. The television is infuriating after the second ad. I stare at the blank canvas in front of me with my brush in hand, but nothing wants to come through. My tea grew cold after I forgot it was sitting on top of my nightstand. I follow the moon's movement from my window to see where it decides to go, and I try to see how many stars and planets I can spot. Sixty-two, but the sky is constantly changing. I count backward. I count sheep. I even try to rock myself to sleep, but everything I do gives me more energy than before. And it all boils down to one name I whisper aloud into the void.

"Ruby."

How long has it been since last I saw her blue eyes shimmering like a river against her blue-black skin?

"You know you used to call her name in your sleep when we first got together." I almost jump out of my skin as I turn to find Roy lying next to me in bed.

"Jesus Roy, you know you can't just pop up like that!"

"Now you know when I'm gonna pop up, woman. I'm you." I sit up and push the blanket to my feet.

"Oh right. Maybe I just need someone to talk to. How come you didn't tell me that back then?"

He shrugs and starts picking his teeth like he always did whenever he wanted to avoid a conversation.

"Honestly, I never thought nothin' of it. I thought it was a cousin or friend or somethin' like that." He stops picking his teeth and looks me in the eyes. "But I guess I was wrong, huh? This Ruby person, had I ever met her?"

"I don't believe so."

"When was the last time you spoke with her?"

"Decades ago. Ruby and I's relationship was always complicated. She was my best friend."

"From the way you been tossin' and turnin' all night, seems like she was more than just your best friend. And I thought I knew all your friends."

"I told you it was complicated. And I didn't have to tell you everything about my life. I'm sure you didn't tell me everything about yours."

"I'm sure I probably did. But that's where we're different. I didn't keep any secrets from you, Peach."

"Oh yeah, well what about the war? You didn't tell me what really happened over there."

"That's different. I was trying to spare you the nightmares that comes with knowing those stories."

I pull the blanket back over my legs, suddenly freezing.

"Did you love her?"

I say nothing. I can't. Of course I loved her. She was my first love. But what good would it do to talk to my dead husband about my first love?

"I'm so sorry, Roy." My voice trembles, as tears and guilt bubble up inside me.

"What you got to be sorry about? You're right. We both had a past before each other. The love we had was one for the books. And perhaps the love you had for Ruby, is it?" I nod.

"Maybe that love was one for the books too. Just looks like it never got the chance to have a final chapter."

"But that was just a fling here and there. I'm not really attracted to women. I was with you for over fifty years."

He lays back on the bed, crosses his feet, and places his hands behind his head.

"You know, I've learned a lot of things since being dead. And one of those things is that you can try to trick the mind with all your rational thinking, but you can never trick the heart. The body's not as complicated as you think, Peach. It knows. And it sounds like you've been successful at deceiving yourself for a long time."

What if I want to continue tricking my mind? What if I need to keep telling myself that Ruby was just a thing of the past? Like an old habit that took years to break. It would be a lot easier than admitting I had buried a part of myself so deep I don't recognize when it's staring me in the face. There's also a small part of me that wants Roy to be more upset. Deep down, I want my guilt to be validated. I want to throw myself a pity party for the rest of the night after being scolded by Roy for keeping such a big secret from him. Would he be this calm if I were calling another man's name out in bed when I slept? Would he have waited to bring it up in the afterlife? Guess it doesn't matter now. This line of thinking will not serve my plan to reclaim my life.

I tiptoe to the computer at my desk as if I were sneaking through the front door of my mother's house after coming home from somewhere I knew I shouldn't have been. The creaking of the hickory floorboards makes me jumpy, and the hot air blowing out of the fan is only increasing my irritation. I can't understand why I'm going through so much trouble stirring up something that ought to remain buried within the soil of my mind. Seventy-five is not the time for me to be planting those types of seeds. The first thing I type into Google is, How do I know if I'm gay? I look over my shoulders, expecting someone to be there, but the only presence in the room with me is my own judgment. The number of results surprises me. Is everyone gay? Because looking at how many results there are makes me think everyone just may be. Or perhaps curious. There are articles, personal stories, and videos. All are very informative, but none give the answer I'm searching for.

I can tell I've been at it for a few hours just by looking outside my window and hearing the rustling of birds as they prepare to wake. It's three in the morning. I would always wake up around this time to paint. My internal clock has been waking me up at three since I was a child. My mother would hear me moving around in my room and storm in with her Bible in hand and grab me by the forearm.

***

"Why are you up at this time of the morning?" she demanded.

"I'm not tired no more," I said with sleep still in my eyes.

"Do you know what happens to little girls who wake up at this time?"

I shook my head no, more frightened by my mother's grip and the wild look in her eyes than the story she was about to tell me.

"Demons and spirits alike come and claim their souls. At night you're only protected in the dream world when you sleep. But when you wake up, you become theirs. Especially at three in the mornin' when they're the most active."

"Is that true?"

"You wanna stay up and find out?"

I shook my head no again.

"Good. Now put your hand on this Bible, so I can pray over you. Lord knows how long you've been wakin' up doin' this."

It wasn't until my mother died that I stopped forcing myself to stay in bed at three. It became my favorite time of the day, the time when I would get the most work done. But as I sit at my desk staring at the computer screen and clicking from page to page, I no longer know if I'm being productive in my search or if I'm down a rabbit hole. My eleven-year-old grandson, Luke, taught me that saying a while back when I couldn't stop watching YouTube videos. My eyes ache. I want to close them and welcome temporary darkness, but my mind is too wired.

After reading through several articles, I find myself on a website offering a quiz I can take to tell me what my sexuality is.

"Finally, something useful," I say aloud.

I spend around twenty minutes taking a ten-question quiz. Each question prolongs the process as it takes me back to old memories.

***

Ruby and I were sixteen when we smoked our first cigarette. I stole a pack and lighter from my mom, who smoked more than a chimney. We ran off in the early morning when the sky was changing from indigo to a warm, pinkish orange. The air smelled of sweet dew and burning leaves somewhere in the distance. Sunrise was our favorite time of the day to be together and the only time when people weren't at the lake swimming.

We sat on the dock with our feet in the cold water, something we had been doing since we were little girls. I pulled the pack of cigarettes out of my back pocket.

"Are you sure we're not gonna get in trouble?" Ruby asked with real fear in her eyes. Knowing the type of household she grew up in and how mean her father and stepmother were, I understood. Ruby's fear was her body's way of protecting her. My mother was far from being as sweet as pie, making it easier for me to relate. I knew the meaning of survival very well.

"We're not gonna get in trouble. We're just gonna take one puff to see if we like it. If we do, we can go in the bathrooms at school and smoke with the other girls."

"And if we don't?"

I shrugged with a cigarette dangling from my lips.

"We just won't smoke with them. Ready?"

Ruby nodded and I lit the tip as my mother had done hundreds of times since I was born. The smoke from my long inhale hit the back of my throat like broken glass. Regaining my breath while keeping my composure took everything within me. I passed the cigarette to Ruby, who took it with shaking hands.

"It's not that bad, really," I said in between coughs. "I think we just gotta get used to it."

Ruby inhaled from the same cigarette my lips had held and started her own coughing fit. We laughed and kept trying, ignoring the burning sensation in our throats and lungs, and focusing all of our attention on how sophisticated we looked.

"Okay, let me try something," Ruby said. "I'm gonna inhale, and you're gonna open your mouth, and I'm gonna blow the smoke in your mouth."

It seemed like a strange thing for her to suggest, but I did it anyway. It was, however, the first time I ever noticed how round and full Ruby's lips were. They were dark-brown on the top and more pink on the bottom. The thought of possibly kissing her flashed through my mind. I jumped back from fear that she could read my thoughts. I later found out that Ruby was thinking about the same thing.

***

The sun will rise soon, and I have reached two conclusions about my web search. One, there are entirely too many results and too many opinions in this world. I don't know how people find anything these days. And two, I don't know if I'm gay, bisexual, something called pansexual, fluid, or queer. I honestly don't know what three of those identities fully mean, but I do know that everything I thought I knew about myself is only half the truth.

***

After getting roughly four hours of sleep, I wake up around eight the next morning, groggy but determined. It's my second day of putting my awakening plan into action, and I don't want to waste any time. Instead of my usual toast, banana, and green tea for breakfast, I'm going to eat some cookie dough ice cream hidden in the back of my freezer. I only eat dessert on special occasions. Today, I'm eating it straight from the carton. There's no time for diets on a journey of living to the fullest, and ice cream is a small feat compared to some of the other things I'm preparing to tackle. But I'm tackling it one scoop at a time. Besides, I'm tired of everyone under the age of fifty telling me I need to make sure I'm eating properly to stay fit, healthy, and live a long life.

"I must be doing somethin' right if I made it this far. Maybe they should be asking me for health advice, not the other way around."

I gaze out the window at the school buses going by with my cold, sweet spoon sitting comfortably in my mouth.

I take off my house shoes and wiggle my toes on the hard, bare floor. There are so many rules to follow to be a proper lady. Eat this many calories. Exercise this many times a week. Never walk barefoot. Always be seen, not heard. Marry by this age. Have children by that age. Learn how to sleep pretty so you don't mess up your hair. They could make a book the size of fifty encyclopedias of rules girls and women are to follow.

Now that I'm older, there seem to be even more unspoken rules. Don't wear clothes that are too revealing or too flashy. Don't go out alone. Don't have sex. Don't think about sex. In fact, the only thing an older woman is allowed to do is sit comfortably in a chair, knit or read, and reflect on the life she lived.

The coldness of the ice cream sliding down my throat and the chilly morning floor waking up my toes feel so good that a tiny moan escapes from my lips. When was the last time I moaned? It's a shame I can't recall, because I am excellent at it. But again, I fell into the trap of getting older in this society. Even moaning is for the young.

After enjoying a morning doing nothing but lounging around the house, I call up Destiny and ask her to stop by after her classes. Destiny is such a smart girl and the most helpful out of my two grands. I will never admit this to anyone and will swear up and down that it is not true, but Destiny is my favorite out of the grands and my child. I wait for her on the porch while listening to the birds singing and children playing in the street. The flowers, herbs, and vegetables are growing slowly in my garden. If I listen hard enough, I can hear the bees land on my black-eyed Susans as the ladybugs climb a stalk of mint. The porch is one of my favorite things about this house and the reason I chose this place when Roy and I were house hunting in our twenties. Back then, I could picture myself watching and listening in the same way the women used to do in my hometown. Someone was always on their porch, talking, staring at you from afar, inviting you to come and have a glass of sweet tea, getting on you for doing something you weren't supposed to be doing or being somewhere you weren't supposed to be. The porch was a sign of community. The porch was my symbol of home.

A red car pulls up to the front of the house right as my eyes get comfortable enough in the sun to let me fall asleep. Destiny hops out of the car with a basket in her hand.

"Well, hello there, Grandmother."

"Well, hello there, Destiny. Is that for *moi*?"

She sits next to me and hands me the basket.

"But of course. I got so many seeds in class today. We had a guest lecturer who runs her own farm, and she brought some packs for everyone to take with them. Of course I had to grab as many as I could for you."

I pat her leg. "That a girl. I can start planting some of these today."

"So, what was so urgent I needed to come over after class?"

"I can't just want to see my granddaughter?"

"Yes, and you do every Saturday. Today is Tuesday, meaning there must be something on your mind."

I look out at my garden, resting my hands on my rising and falling stomach.

"Have you ever watched birds?"

Destiny follows my eyes. "I don't think I have. I like to listen to them in the morning."

"I've been coming out here, year-round, since your grandad and I first moved into this house. The first thing I loved to do here, before the garden, was watching the birds. No one has to tell birds to fly. Or when they need to build a nest. No one tells them when to mate. Or how they should take care of their offspring. Or where they should go in this world. They just do it. They don't need permission to live. I've always envied them for that."

"Grandma, you don't need permission to live either." Destiny places her hand on top of mine.

"Yeah, I'm remembering that now."

"Is that why you called me over, to watch birds?"

"Don't be silly." I turn to face my granddaughter with hesitancy, mainly to give myself more time to think about what exactly I want to say.

"Grandma, you're scaring me. Are you okay? What's wrong?"

I can see in Destiny's eyes her thoughts have gone where most younger people's thoughts go when an older person has something important to tell them. Either I'm sick, injured, dying, or a combination of all three. I pat her hand for reassurance.

"Don't let your imagination run so wild. I'm not goin' nowhere yet. But I do have something to tell you, and you must promise not to tell anyone until I'm ready." Destiny zips her lips like she used to do when I would sneak her extra candy to take home with her.

"You're still a gender and sexuality studies major, right?"

She nods. "Yeah, I'm surprised you remembered. Everyone else in our family gets amnesia when it comes to my major. I think they're just hoping I'll change it. But what about it?"

I straighten out the wrinkles in my sage, linen pants. "Well, I'm a woman and I need you to study my sexuality."

Destiny looks at me with all the confusion I'm feeling on the inside.

"What do you mean by sexuality?"

Remember your plan, Juliet. Just tell her. Ignore the ice cream in your belly threatening to make a warm reappearance. Without letting her get a word in, I tell Destiny about my awakening plan that led me to see the Italian movie on my birthday and about the previous night, the articles, stories, and quizzes I took. Finally, I tell her about Ruby. I tell her about our young love and about how confused I am at age seventy-five. Tears form at the bottom of Destiny's eyelids. She's always been sensitive like her mother.

"I'm at a loss for words." She wipes her cheeks.

"Well, I'm sure you'll find them." I laugh, knowing that, also like her mother, she can talk a mile a minute.

"I just always thought Grandad was your first love."

"Why wouldn't you? Your grandad's love was in a category of its own, and so was Ruby's. I've never compared the two, not even now."

"I can't believe you took a quiz to see if you're gay or not. Those quizzes are so bogus. No one can tell you your identity with ten questions. Especially not the internet."

"Yeah, I think I figured that out after the third quiz. But the reason why I asked you to come is that I need your help to find someone."

"Ruby?"

"Yes."

She whips out her phone and starts typing away. I answer all her questions about Ruby to the best of my ability. I don't know where she lives. I don't know if her last name has changed or if she's on the internet. I also don't know if Ruby wants to be found or if she is still alive. The unknown is making my head spin. My arms are covered in chills, my stomach twisted in a knot, and my heart is speeding up with every passing second. The giddiness and headache that comes with love. My fear melts into my excitement, and my excitement melts into my anxiety. There's no separation between any of my emotions. All I want is for Destiny's fingers to stop typing and for her to look up and say she found Ruby.

"There's nothing here. It's almost like she doesn't even exist. And here I thought old people loved Facebook."

My excitement fades. "Apparently not all of us."

Destiny places her hand on mine once more. Apparently, I didn't hide the disappointment in my voice. I return to watching the birds.

"Don't worry, Grandma. I'm gonna keep looking for her. Just because she's not popping up right away doesn't mean I can't find something on her. Sometimes it's harder to find things when you're looking too closely."

"No, you're right. If we're meant to find her, we will. In the meantime, there's another favor I wanted to ask you."

"Of course, anything."

"I need to explore my sexuality more, and I need your help."

Destiny doesn't say anything for a while.

"What do you want me to do?"

"Well, you're the progressive one in the family. You have all those colorful friends. Introduce me to them. Let me sit at the feet and soak in some of the wisdom you young people have."

Destiny smiles. "That's a great idea. How about this? If you're up for it, there's a party coming up. It's very *colorful,* as you say. I think you'll enjoy it."

I turn back to the birds. "I think so too."

Chapter Three

I FIRST MET RUBY on a Friday afternoon in the town center. I was supposed to be at school, and my mother was supposed to be at work. That morning, she grabbed my hand and winked at me. "Playin' hooky every once in a while ain't gonna kill nobody. Today it'll just be me and you."

I was seven, before my father's affair and before the bitterness ate away at my mother. My mother was the type who enjoyed cooking big meals and sewing dresses with crooked seams for me to wear to school and church. She was the type who hummed softly to herself as she parted my hair on Saturday afternoons. I often peeked from my room, as she giggled like a schoolgirl when my daddy pulled her into his arms and slow danced to whatever was playing on their old radio. If I had known how our relationship would change, I would've savored those words on that Friday afternoon as if they were my last meal or last breath.

We walked past shops filled with pretty dresses, hats, purses, and shoes. I was little, but like most children, I was very observant, especially of my parents. I could tell by the way my mother's eyes twinkled at the sight of all the pretty things in the windows and how she stared longingly at the white women in the shops trying on all those pretty things, that she wished she were in there.

"Ain't that something, those poor dresses? They have no one to fill 'em out and wiggle around in them. Not enough hips." A tall, slender-yet-hipty woman with dark-brown skin and blue eyes looked down at me and winked. She was the most beautiful woman I had ever seen. She looked like she was going to an important meeting dressed in a jade-colored dress and a matching hat with lace that swooped right above her right eye. She held a tiny purse in one hand and the hand of a little girl who looked just like her in the other.

My mother laughed at the boldness of the woman. "It's a shame. I know a whole bunch of women who would do those dresses justice. Me included."

"I knew you had an eye for fashion. That's why I had to stop. It's settled. You're gonna have to come on over to my house on Fridays to join me and some other ladies at our sewing night."

"Oh, I'm not the best sewer. My mama never took the time to really teach me." My usually confident mother looked as if she were a little girl standing next to the woman who exuded more confidence than the sun.

"Don't you worry about that. I'm one of the best seamstresses in town. I've even sewed stuff for those women in there. I'll teach you. There's nothing like making dresses for women who know how to wear them, if you get my drift. I'm Maybelle, by the way, but people call me May. And this is my Ruby."

"It's nice to meet you, May. I'm Claudine, and this is my daughter, Juliet." May wrote down directions to her house on a tiny piece of paper and gave it to my mother.

"Bring your little girl with you when you come. I have a feeling our girls are gonna become really good friends."

***

Not only did Ruby and I become good friends, our mothers became almost inseparable after that day. We spent nearly every weekend at one another's houses, sitting on porches, sewing dresses, gossiping about everyone in town. But two years later, Ruby's mother passed away in a train accident on her way to New York for a sewing gig. Her father remarried one of the meanest women in town. My mother no longer had a best friend, but Ruby and I remained joined at the hips. If you saw one of us, you saw the other. We became each other's refuge.

It wasn't until the summer of 1963 that our friendship changed. The rain was constant that year, making the days feel short. Ruby and I were fifteen. Our days spent playing with dolls and hosting tea parties were now spent listening to records and practicing new dance moves. Ruby's father rarely ever allowed her to go to a dance unless it was at the church. So we spent most of our rainy afternoons in her basement having our own party for two.

"Listen to this new record I heard the other day." Ruby slid the album onto the record player's spindle. Eyes closed, she slowly swayed her hips to the guitar and sang along with Dion's raspy voice.

"It's called 'Ruby Baby.'" I swear he made this song just for me."

"Not with those dance moves."

"Oh, you think you can do better?"

"I know it."

I hopped up and did the monkey and the twist to the song's rhythm. Ruby watched me with a smile.

"What you lookin' at? You forgot how to move your feet?"

Ruby moved closer to me until we were inches away from each other. "You think someone can feel the way they do in that song about me?"

"I don't see why not."

Ruby reached for my hand and touched it softly. "Even if it looks like something you've never seen before?"

"I don't see why not." I repeated, surprised by the closeness of her body to mine. I couldn't figure out why she was staring at me, or why she was biting her bottom lip. I brushed it off as Ruby just being Ruby and went back to dancing until it was time for me to go home.

After that rainy day in the basement, I noticed a difference whenever I was around Ruby. When we were in church singing hymns and trying to keep up with the energy of the choir, Ruby's hand would graze mine. Sometimes quickly. Sometimes slowly. I would lie in my bed at night, staring at the ceiling, replaying every touch, every lingering hug, and each stolen glance. Ruby had been my best friend since we were seven years old. She knew every inch and crevice of the secrets I held. But I wasn't so sure if I knew all her secrets, all her crushes. What puzzled me more than Ruby's odd behavior was the way her eyes made my stomach twist in a knot. Or how deep down, every time her hands touched mine, I wished time would freeze so our hands stayed together for a little longer. I never allowed my thoughts to continue for too long out of fear that God was listening and would somehow, in some way, tell my mother. I would open my Bible on my nightstand, say a few words, and hope that my prayer would be enough to keep me in His good graces...until I closed my eyes and dreamed about how soft

Ruby's lips would be if they just so happened to press against mine.

With each passing day, Ruby grew bolder. Her hand lingered longer. Her body moved closer to mine. We sat on the dock one day after school, trying to spot fish in the lake. Her hand rested on top of mine.

I moved my hand away. "Okay, what's up with you?"

"What do you mean?"

"You know what I mean, Ruby. The touching, the staring. You've been acting strange since that day in your basement."

"You never told me to stop."

"That's because I don't know what you're doing! Or why you're doing it."

She turned her body to face mine and looked me directly in the eyes.

"Don't you feel it?"

"Feel what?" I asked.

"The spark. Between us. It feels like more than just friendship."

She was right. There was something between us that did feel like more, but I had no clue what that more was.

"I was confused at first too. But the more time we spent together the more I wanted to be around you, to touch you...and kiss you."

"Kiss me?" My thoughts jumped back to the recurring dreams I'd been having of her.

She leaned in and gently pressed her lips to mine. It was exactly like my dreams. Except she tasted like oranges, and I had no idea what to do with the rest of my body. I didn't know if I should move my hands. I wondered if I should wrap my arms around her and move my head from side to side like in the movies. Before I could make up my mind, the kiss was over.

"So?"

"So, what?"

"Did you like it? Was it too strange for you?"

"No, it wasn't strange at all. It was kinda nice."

"Do you think this is going to ruin our friendship?" she asked, as she played with the rings on my fingers.

"I hope not."

"Let's make a vow. No matter what happens, no matter if we're romantic with each other and it doesn't work out in the end, we'll always remain best friends."

We held out our pinkies and interlocked them.

"Deal, no matter what happens." I hoped it would be the truth.

***

Between 1963 and 1964, my blossoming first love was as sweet as honeysuckle. It was easy to fall for Ruby. It was easy to hold her hand in secret at the library after school. It was easy to pass notes back and forth during choir practice. It was even easy to dream up a world in the future that was filled with more moments of us, Juliet and Ruby. But there can never be ease without complications. Ours came after our high school graduation, when it was time for us to go off to college.

Southern Georgia was in the midst of tornado season, which meant severe thunderstorms came often. The humidity always made our fresh-pressed hair wither like a rose in the desert. We met up at the dock as planned, Ruby and me. She was wearing a blue sundress that stopped right at her thigh. The air smelled of rain, and a hint of the rose perfume Ruby always dabbed on the nape of her neck. She was holding a blue umbrella to match her dress, and a rain cap to protect her freshly straightened and curled hair. With her bare feet and half smile, Ruby was the most beautiful person I had ever seen. I wanted to paint her, so I wouldn't forget how she looked standing in the rain with trees swaying behind her. It was as if the whole world was dancing to both of us, to our love, our youth, to the time we spent at the lake, judged by no one.

"There you are, always late. We're gonna miss the train if you don't hurry up." Ruby's eyes landed on my empty hand.

"Where's your bag?"

"I..."

"What, a cat got your tongue? Come on now, stop playing. We're gonna be late."

"I can't go." I wasn't sure she heard my faint whisper over the rain, wind, and crashing leaves, but she did.

"What do you mean you can't go?"

"I can't go, Ruby."

"Why not? We both got accepted into Spelman. We had it all planned out. We were gonna leave and start a life together where no one knows us, remember?" I remembered. I remembered all our conversations. I'd been a part of the dreaming process just as much as she had. I planted the seed. Watered it daily. No one could've told me I would be the one to chop the stem before the flower had a chance to bloom. I stuffed my hands in the pockets of a pair of old overalls my dad had given me. Ruby was dressed to meet the world. I looked like someone who'd remain stuck in our town. For a moment, I tried convincing myself she didn't deserve to be with someone like me.

"My mother is sick. They don't know what it is, but they don't think she's gonna live long." Tears filled the bottom of my eyelids.

"So, you're gonna stay here with her? The main person you were trying to get away from?"

"If I don't stay, who will? All she got is me."

"What about your dreams of being a famous painter, and me being a teacher and writer, us getting a house together even if people only referred to us as roommates? We were gonna be roommates for the rest of our lives."

"I can't leave her here by herself, Ruby. I'll still be a painter. You'll still be a teacher and writer. Maybe one day, when she's better, we can meet up and get that house and become those roommates. But I could never forgive myself if I left her like this, knowing that she's gonna be by herself." Tears ran down both of our faces, mixing with the tears falling from the sky.

"You're not gonna come visit me in Atlanta. Weeks will go by, and you'll be busy being the good daughter your mother does not deserve. Eventually, months will go by. We'll send letters to keep each other up-to-date about our lives. But those letters will become a reminder of how different our lives are becoming. You'll meet someone, or I'll meet someone. And our friendship and love will be forced to move aside to make room for someone new. And life will go on."

I didn't want to believe anything she was saying, but I also believed in signs, ever since I was a little girl. The wind whipping through the trees and the slanted rain crashing into the lake was all the confirmation I needed. I knew, at that moment, God or Spirit or whoever was watching us was speaking to me. But I didn't know quite what God was trying to say. We stood in silence, rain drowning our thoughts. Neither one of us had any words left to fill the space between us. I hadn't said much, but every word I did say made it feel like a stack of bricks was being piled onto my back, one by one. Ruby grabbed her suitcase and walked in the direction of the train station. Seconds went by before I built up the nerve to call out to her. I had to stop her, tell her I loved her and that she was my best friend. When I turned around, she had already turned the corner and disappeared into the trees. The only thing in front of me was the town I'd decided to stay in.

Chapter Four

MY ORIGINAL PLAN FOR the day was to do absolutely
nothing until it was time for me to go to Lili's house. I've been
soaking in this Epsom-salt bath so long my skin resembles the
prunes my father used to make me eat every morning.
Mentally, I'm exhausted. The rain has been beating on the
windows and roof since I first got out of bed. Although my body
wants to get back under that blanket and stay curled up, my
mind wants a change of scenery.

I grab a yellow umbrella by the front door, lock up the house,
and catch a glimpse of a bird taking shelter beneath the canopy
of the trees. Birds don't overthink about where they should go
and where they shouldn't go. They go wherever they please. "So
just go, Juliet, and stop thinking so much!" I listen to the sound
of the water splattering beneath my feet.

"Hey lady watch out for that puddle!"

I barely hear the warning from across the street before
finding myself ankle deep in cold rainwater.

"Tried to warn ya." I faintly hear the person murmur as they
walk away. I look down at the small pool of water beneath me.
When was the last time my feet were in a puddle? When I was
seven? Ten?

I wish I could blame my age for this occurrence. Something,
anything outside of myself that I could put all my guilt into and
hold it up and say, "This is to blame for why I haven't been
living my life the way I wanted to. It has nothing to do with me.
It has to do with this thing!"

Of course, the only tangible thing I must blame is myself. So
here I am at seventy-five, throwing myself the pity party I've
been craving. I continue walking, while imagining a cloud is
right above me, punishing me for taking life for granted.
There's comfort in my pity. Where the notion came from that
older people must have their lives all figured out is beyond me.
I have nothing figured out—especially not my life.

Whenever I'm in one of my grey moods, there's always one person I can think of to make me feel better, my father. Andy Rollings was kind to everyone he met, but he never hid his flaws from me. He would always say, from the time I was a little girl to when he was on his dying bed, "Now look here, I may be your father, but I am only a man."

Even as a young child, I knew exactly what he was trying to say. His admission shaped the way I view and interact with others. He wasn't perfect, no matter how high of a pedestal I held him on. Andy Rollings was a great father but a horrible husband. He sucked the life force out of my mother, and she was never able to recover. My mother gave everything to her marriage, to be a doting wife and mother who was always active in the church and community. When her perfect image shattered, she lost herself. I swore to myself, at a young age, I would never get married. I never wanted to look in the mirror and see a ghost of who I once was. Little did I know that's exactly what would happen.

The rain starts to slack off just as I reach the end of my street. It feels like I've been walking for hours, but I'm only a few doors down from my house. My pants and shoes are soaked. I used to love jumping in puddles as a child, especially after a thunderstorm. There's a puddle in front of me that's making my stomach clench in excitement like it did when I was seven. I stop thinking, lift my shoe, and stomp in the sitting water. First, I stomp softly, afraid someone may be watching me. Then I forget about that imaginary someone and stomp with both feet until the pity tears stinging my eyes turn into laughter. I'm laughing and stomping in the muddy water, when a black car pulls up beside me.

"Ma? What are you doing?"

For a moment, I forget where I am. I'm not a mother. I'm not a grandmother or an artist. I forget all the identities I hold close to my heart. So when I hear someone calling me Ma, I don't respond right away. How can I? I'm no one's ma. They're not talking to me. I keep stomping until the strange voice calls me again.

"Mom, get in the car. People are looking!"

I glance over at the car to find Toni and Destiny staring at me. My identities return, and conflicting feelings of embarrassment and freedom wash over my body, sending a shiver up from my toes to my ears. I get into the car without saying a word, my eyes never leaving the small, muddy puddle. That body of water is still wiggling from a woman who got out of her mind long enough to return to her body. It was like dancing. Passionate lovemaking. Or the cookies and cream ice cream I ate earlier this week straight from the carton. All I want is for that woman to stick around.

Once we return home, no one says anything about me playing in a puddle like a child. I take my sweet time changing out of my wet clothes, put on a blues record, and place a kettle on the stove to boil. Both Toni and Destiny are silent as they watch me move around the house. I know what they're thinking. They want to see if they notice anything off about me. Am I forgetting what I'm doing, will I remember to turn off the stove? Do I remember who they are, and how often do I wander around the neighborhood stomping in puddles? It was like nothing they had ever seen before. Throughout the years, I've become a professional at appearing put together. I left my days of rebelling against the world back in my twenties. Or so I thought.

"Will you two quit staring at me?" I carry a tray with three mugs of tea to the kitchen table where they're sitting. Judging.

"Why weren't you picking up your phone?" Toni gets straight to the point.

"I left it here."

"What if something happened? What if you needed to call us?"

"I was outside. If something were to happen, someone would've eventually seen me." I raise my tea to my lips, breathing in the fresh aroma of lemongrass.

"So you're going to leave your life in someone else's hands?"

"Was there anything I could help you two with? Because I have to start getting ready. I'm going out soon."

"We were just worried about you. Mom tried calling, and then of course she called me. Then I tried calling you. When I told her you didn't pick up, I couldn't stop her. So here we are. We just wanted to make sure you're okay." Destiny looks at me, waiting for a response. I don't give her one.

"You are okay, right?"

My patience is wearing thin the longer I look at my descendants. Who gave them the right to treat me like a child, checking in on me every two seconds? If I want to jump in puddles and parade around the house butt naked, I have the right to do so. And I don't owe anyone an explanation.

"It was nice for you two to stop by and check on me. As you can see, I'm fine, but I do have plans. So if you will excuse me. Y'all know your way out."

I walk to my room, close the door, and don't leave until I hear Destiny call out, "We're leaving, Grandma. We'll call you tomorrow!"

Finally, I'm alone again. It's the second best feeling I've had all day.

Chapter Five

LILI'S LIVING ROOM SMELLS of liquor, perfume, and her Puerto Rican cooking. *Empanadillas, asopao de gandules, bacalaitos*, the usual. She goes all out when it comes to parties; cooking is her love language. I always come prepared to be stuffed. The lights are bright, and the round table is already set up for the game in the living room. I'm grateful for the invitation, for a chance to be around women my age.

"Don't get scared on me now, Shirley! Because that book is mine, thank you!" Lili reaches across the table to give me a high five.

"How many books are those, Juls?"

"Six."

"Y'all are about to be set! Come on!"

Shirley and Victoria, whom I've just met, give each other the biggest eye rolls they can muster.

"How come there's never any men here?" Shirley asks.

"If you know some, invite them." Lili shuffles the cards.

Victoria turns to me. "Do you know any, Juliet?"

"Not at the moment, no."

Do I know any men? The question should've been, do I want to know any men? Or where would I even find them? Would I ever be able to avoid comparing another man to Roy? I always wonder how older widows find love again. How could they possibly have room in their hearts for someone else at their age? How can those new men or women compete against a lifetime? There's never anyone to answer any of my questions. Maybe it's because I'm not asking them aloud.

"Well I think I'm gonna start playing cards at the senior center instead of with you old broads," Shirley says.

Lili slaps down one of her cards in the middle of the table. "Oh hush. You only start talking like that when y'all are losing. Which is every time, so just get over it. You're not goin' anywhere."

"Actually, I just might be going somewhere." Shirley takes a sip of her wine.

"Where?" Victoria asks.

"My son wants me to live at Spring Oaks."

"The retirement community! Oh no, tell your son to take that bullshit to someone else and tell him it came from me." Lili slaps her hand on the table.

"I agree," Victoria chimes in.

I remain quiet. It's like watching a dramatic film.

"I can't do that. He's been paying my bills for the past three years, and he feels that I would be happier somewhere where there are people my age."

"Or he saw how all these new people are moving into this neighborhood, and he got a good deal to sell the house. My son called me last week telling me that if I sold the house, we would be set for years," Lili says.

"What did you tell him?" Victoria asks.

"I told him if he wanted to be set for life, he should take his grown ass down to the unemployment office. I am not proud to say that I raised the laziest son in the world."

"You know what, I'm tired of our children thinking they have a right to dictate what we do and don't do with our life. My daughter and granddaughter came by today, and they kept looking at me as if they were waiting for a hip to pop out or for me to forget who they were. My brain is sharper than it was thirty years ago. I'm not suffering from an aching body every day. I'm not losing my mind. Sometimes it's exhausting to constantly be reminded that you are no longer young." I don't mention the part about my plan, or stomping in a puddle, or about Ruby. But none of it matters, because by the way everyone's head is nodding, I said exactly what they were all thinking. Lili lifts her glass.

"I couldn't have said it better myself. Fuck our noisy, entitled offspring! Fuck being young! Here's to living without giving a damn." We all clink our glasses together, but I can tell Shirley isn't as enthusiastic about what's being said. Shirley's voice is lower than it was before but still steady as she speaks.

"Earl and I loved our house. But Earl's not here. It's just me. I'm not some poor old woman who doesn't have a say. I'm tired of living alone. I'm tired of waiting around my house for something, anything to happen. I spend most of my days watching television. The best part of my week can't be to come here and play cards. I *want* to go to Spring Oaks. I want to have a social life. I want to meet men. I want to possibly have sex again. Or at least have someone nibble on my ear every once in a while."

We're both on a journey to overcome the same beast, loneliness. I get where she's coming from. Although I don't want to spend my years in a retirement community, I don't want to spend the rest of my years alone either.

"I heard that Spring Oaks is a lovely place to live. I've met many people who live there, and they love it. I think you'll enjoy it." I smile at Shirley, who returns my smile with what I believe is a deep sense of gratitude.

We play cards for hours, while talking and drinking more glasses of alcohol than we should. The more wine that slithers through our bloodstream, the more comfortable we become with one another. It's always a good time to sit around with a group of women telling jokes we have no business telling. Dirty jokes. The kind that's only told when no one is around. Fantasies. The ones that make you cross your legs just from thinking about them. When women can gather without feeling they're being watched or judged, they can let their breasts hang low, and their mouths run wild. And that's exactly what we do.

"I had this one dream the other night about my next-door neighbor, Mr. Carmichael. Now I knew it was a dream because I've never been that flexible in my life." Lili tries to show what exactly happened between her and Mr. Carmichael.

"Well, that's not worse than me sitting at church on Sunday a couple of weeks ago. My phone was at the bottom of my purse, on my lap. Pastor William was looking extra fine and glistening from his sweat, and I forgot to turn off an alarm on my phone." Victoria fans her red face.

"What did you do?" I ask.

"I kept on letting it vibrate. Hell, it felt kind of good. For a minute or two, it was just me and the pastor in that church, if you get my drift."

"Didn't anyone tell you to turn off your phone?" Shirley asks.

"Of course not. How would it look to tell your elder to turn off their phone? Besides, if anyone would've said something, I would've just blamed it on one of the young folks around me."

We all laugh until our bellies ache and tears sting our eyes. It's euphoric to be seen and understood. It feels like the sensation that washes over the body after a good cry or even a wonderful orgasm. And there's an unspoken understanding that our words will never leave Lili's kitchen table.

Once I'm back at my house, I'm a little tipsy but filled with a surge of creativity. I walk into my art studio and light candles throughout the room to create a soft glow. This used to be Toni's room, but Roy converted it not long after she moved out and got married. It's my favorite room in the house. A big window overlooks the second garden and a small pond in the backyard. I always spot deer, rabbits, and birds of all shapes and sizes. There's a large oak tree I never tire of watching transition through the seasons. I loved rocking Toni to sleep in the rocking chair while watching the snow blanket the earth during the winter months. I used to enjoy forcing Roy to pose for me when I would practice painting portraits. My art supplies are covered in dust. It's been a while. Existential dread isn't always the best for creativity. But I'm feeling a spark, and I won't be able to sleep until I paint something, anything.

After hours of painting intensely, a beautiful image of a lotus flower floating on a lake emerges on the canvas. I step back as my mind drifts to when I first saw a lotus flower in a book.

***

Ruby and I were sixteen. We had been sneaking off to the dock to steal kisses under the rising sun. We didn't know what we were doing, nor did we have a name for it. But it was so tender and soft that it couldn't have been anything else but young love. I was painting a portrait of Ruby. We were on the dock on a Sunday morning, when we should've been at church. We understood we would get in trouble for skipping church, but that type of trouble was good trouble. It was the type of trouble we were willing to get in just to spend a few extra moments together, alone. As I painted underneath a cloudy sky next to the murky lake water, I kept getting stuck on Ruby's eyes. No matter what I did, I couldn't get the color just right. Ruby was reading a book she'd found hidden underneath her brother's bed, *Giovanni's Room* by James Baldwin, oblivious to my frustration. When she finally looked up at me, time had stopped for the both of us. The way the sun caught hold of the blueness in Ruby's eyes was like nothing I had ever seen. I had to remind myself to breathe.

"You know your eyes are like water, mine are like mud, and you know what type of flower grows from that?"

"Oh gosh, you and your flowers." Ruby playfully rolled her eyes.

"You wanna know or not?"

"I'm just joking. What flower grows from the water and dirt, besides all of them?"

"A lotus flower. I read it in some book at the library. It can grow in the muddiest place and produce a beautiful flower on top of the water. They're the most beautiful flowers I've ever seen."

***

I used to paint lotus flowers all the time. Whenever I was feeling lonely or sad, or when I wanted to remind myself of something beautiful and innocent, of Ruby, I would pull out my blue watercolor paints. Many of those paintings were lost with time. Some I kept stored away with my other old paintings. Except for one. Roy thought his favorite would fit perfectly in our bathroom. I'm usually against hanging up my artwork, but he was so excited I couldn't say no.

"So this is the real meaning of the lotus flower?" Roy appears to the left of me and my daydream fades away. He's leaning against the windowsill with an unlit cigarette hanging from his mouth, watching me.

"And here I am, all this time, thinking that it had something to do with me goin' to Vietnam."

I set my paintbrush down. "What are you over there yappin' about?"

He looks at me without saying anything for a long time. It's unnerving to have someone stare at me for so long, especially when it's someone who knows me better than most. He clenches his jaw. I can see tiny veins popping out of his forehead. What is he mad about? I did nothing wrong.

"When I found that painting you told me you painted it for me."

"I did no such thing! You just assumed I painted it for you."

"Well, you didn't correct me! I thought that flower reminded you of me, Peach. I thought you painted it when I was off in a war, trying to survive for this damn country. You were always researching something, so I figured you had done research on Vietnam and found that flower. I used to see them all over, and all I could think about when I saw them was you. Out of all the horrendous things I saw, that lotus was the beauty that kept me going. And when I got back and saw your painting, I knew I had made the right decision to commit my life to you. I knew it was fate. But really that painting was for her, wasn't it?"

"What do you want me to say, huh? Sorry? I'm not sorry, Roy. I can't change the past. I'm just trying to learn how to accept it now. And don't you dare try to accuse me of not thinking of you while you were gone. I was young. And might I remind you, we were not married yet. So if you're looking for me to stroke your ego and say sorry, then you came to the wrong place!"

"But you *are* tryna change the past. That's why you're lookin' for her."

A tree branch hits the window behind me. Startled, I knock over the jar of water on the stool. The water's color is a mix of blue and green, like the ocean. It looks like her eyes. When I turn back around to the window, Roy is gone. I'm left with a deeply rooted anger at myself for not telling him about the hidden things in my life before he became a part of my inner world.

I walk outside to get some fresh air. I pull my jacket tighter across my body and stare at the front of my house. The house is barely visible in the dark, but I know each nook and cranny like the back of my hand. The red brick lining the bottom of my Craftsman-style home. The vines crawling up the left side of the house. The bats that love to fly back and forth from my chimney to the neighbor's. I know all the rhythms. For some reason, I don't want to walk back through that front door. Did Roy's words upset me so much that I don't even want to go back into my own home? No, it's not Roy. It's me. Why should I walk back into that house? Whenever I try moving one foot forward, something stops me from taking another step. I don't want to go to my room, take a shower, and go to bed. I don't want to wake up in the same house and do the same thing I always did.

I pull out my phone with trembling hands and call Destiny, who answers on the first ring.

"Destiny? Hello?"

"Hey Grandma, what's wrong? Are you okay?"

"This is going to sound strange, but I'm standing in front of my house, and I can't go in."

"What do you mean? Did you forget your key?"

"No, I have my key, and I have a spare. I just can't spend the night here tonight. Do you understand?"

"Say no more. You can stay with me tonight. I'm on my way."

I sit on my porch step and look out at the rain hitting the shiny black pavement. It looks like stars falling from the sky and twinkling on the ground. My life feels like those falling stars. Something that was once so beautiful from afar is falling to its rightful place on the earth. Every living thing must return eventually. Those fallen stars, like fallen angels, are the only things keeping me calm while I wait for Destiny to arrive.

Chapter Six

MY MOTHER LEARNED ABOUT Ruby and me before we were supposed to leave for college. Sometimes I think, in some twisted way, she made herself sick just so I wouldn't be happy. She didn't want to see me in love, but she also didn't want anyone in town to find out *who* I was in love with. It would bring shame to the family, to her.

After Ruby left, I spent my days cooking my mother's meals, helping her take her medications, bathing her, feeding her, and cleaning her sheets...all in silence. I never received a thank you. I watched the disease eat away at her body like a vulture eating roadkill, slowly consuming more of her each day. Her cheeks became sunken and her eyes hollowed. The bones protruding out of her once curvaceous flesh took me by surprise. My only distractions were writing letters to Ruby and reading the ones she finally sent me.

> *Dear Ruby,*
>
> *I never wanted to write you letters. I wanted to be right next to you, experiencing a new life away from here. Together. But my mother is dying, Ruby, and even though she doesn't deserve the best mother of the year award she also doesn't deserve to be alone during this time. But I don't want to fill this letter with excuses. I hope, if you ever decide to write back, our letters can make us feel as if we've never left each other's side.*
>
> *Love,*
> *Juliet*

***

> *Dear Juliet,*

*I've received all your letters. I've read each
one many times. I wanted to remain mad at you
for staying. But how can I? I know you better
than most, which means I also know your heart.
I'm no longer angry, and I'm ready to start
fresh. College is a whole new world. There are
all of these traditions we have to do. And I've
met so many girls from all over the country. My
roommate is from New York City! Can you
believe it, New York City? She says I can come
and visit her in the city whenever I want.
Another girl in one of my classes is from
Oklahoma. Not as exciting, but she's a nice girl.
I've met so many wonderful people, and I feel so
grown-up walking around campus. Every step I
take, I think of how my mama once walked this
same path. Anyway, I have to go to chapel. I
miss you, Juliet.*

Love,
Ruby

Sometimes I sent Ruby small paintings I made next to the
lake or in my bedroom, when I wasn't caring for my mother.
Eventually, it became clear we'd taken two different paths. My
letters were only filled with my mother's condition, so I sent
paintings most of the time. Ruby's letters were filled with all her
new experiences at school. She was outgrowing me. I knew it.
So it didn't come as a surprise when I received her last letter.

Dear Juliet,

*I met someone. He's so handsome and comes
from money. I've been going steady with him for
about a month now. Things are getting pretty
serious, and I thought it wouldn't be fair to you
if I continued the letters as if I weren't in a
relationship with someone. I won't be coming
home for Christmas like I said I would in my last
letter. I'm going to meet his parents in Harlem.*

Can you believe that Juliet? I'm going to New York like I've always wanted to! I wish you could come with me. I can just picture you painting a masterpiece and the art world falling head over heels for you. I'm not sure when I'll write again. My feelings for you haven't disappeared, but I think it would be disrespectful to my relationship if we continued our letters. I hope you understand. Who knows? Maybe we'll meet up again down the line. I'll be a well-known writer. You'll be a famous painter. We're bound to see each other again. Take care of yourself, Juliet, with the same intensity you take care of everyone else around you.

> *Sincerely,*
> *Ruby*

I hadn't understood when Ruby stopped ending her letters with "love Ruby." After the last one, I got it loud and clear.

My mother passed away in the early hours of the morning, around three. I should've been grieving. I should've felt like a part of me was now missing, my first home. Instead, my steps felt like I was gliding across the pavement. My chest and heart were lifted to the clouds. I had done all I could to make my mother comfortable during her last days. Now I was free.

It was 1965. I saved my money from cleaning floors and toilets, caring for elderly White people in the nursing home across the tracks, and selling paintings to whoever would buy them. I did whatever I could to make sure I had enough money for a Greyhound ticket from Georgia to California. And to have some left over. I once believed my life was so big and important. From the window of the bus, my town looked small and empty, and my memories faded away to dust. I would miss my dad most of all, but he knew I needed to go. He always knew I needed to go.

"This town isn't big enough for a girl as bright as you," he would whisper whenever my world felt too big to breathe in.

Once I was on the highway, I knew it would be a very long time before I returned to my childhood home.

San Francisco was unlike anything I had ever seen. The ocean, the Golden Gate Bridge, the feeling that one was on the edge of the world and right in the heart of it all at once. I had only really heard about the city once. On the news, at the diner where I worked, they did an exposé on young people moving to the city for new opportunities. There was a stark contrast between my small town and the bustling city. My heart tugged at the image of people walking across the street, going where I didn't know, nor did I care. All I knew was that I wanted to be a part of whatever was going on in that city. I had a cousin, Veronica, living and going to school out there. We hadn't seen each other since we were young girls, but after a conversation between our dads, Veronica offered to let me stay with her. From the moment I walked through Veronica's apartment door, I knew I was home for however long she would keep me.

After having lived in the city for almost a year, I made a small name for myself throughout the bar scene because of my dancing. I never intended to perform at bars. My friend, Tommy, introduced me to the nightlife. I saw that the pay was decent, and it gave me time during the day to work on my art. I figured it wasn't a bad gig. I didn't have to hide like I did with Ruby back home. There were all walks of life in California. In the underground bar world we could be whatever we wanted to be, even if it were only for a night. I loved dancing through the nights with women who loved women and men who loved men.

I was always surrounded by artists, activists, students, and free thinkers who were trying to create a new world. I only thought about home when I called my father. The days of sneaking kisses with Ruby and hiding from my mother felt like a lifetime ago.

I danced on stage wearing nothing but lingerie and a feather boa. The crowd whistled and cheered. I was used to attention from the front-row patrons, but no one could've prepared me for a certain pair of blue eyes watching my every move. The club faded away as my eyes met hers. I tried focusing on the whistles and cheers to keep up my momentum, but my heart thundered in my ears. I struggled to keep my feet moving. I needed to process everything, but I needed the extra money. And I wouldn't throw away a good gig for someone I hadn't heard from in a year. I had moved on and started a new life. I hoped my face didn't give away that I wasn't exactly happy she was right in front of me. By the look on Ruby's face, I knew I wasn't doing a good job of hiding my feelings.

I waited until closing to approach her. All night, she'd sat in the corner of the bar looking uncomfortable around the daring and colorful people in the room. Friday night had turned into four o'clock Saturday morning. There was a quiet bustle in the streets.

"Are you lost?" I asked, outside the bar with a cigarette dangling from my mouth.

"Not exactly. I didn't know you smoked."

"I didn't know you would be in town."

"I thought it could be a surprise. I reached out to your dad, and he gave me your address. I went there first, but Veronica said you were here working tonight. So I figured I'd surprise you."

"Yeah, you said that. You got me. I'm surprised. Now what, you gonna go back home?"

"I can't," she whispered.

"Ruby, I've had a long night. I'm tired. What are you doing here?"

Before I could say anything else, Ruby collapsed to her knees, her back hunched over, her face buried in her hands. Her tears created tiny puddles on the pavement beneath us. The hard exterior I was trying to hold onto instantly dismantled, as my arms wrapped around Ruby the same way they always had since we were little girls.

"I have nowhere to go. I can't go back to him. I can't go back to him."

Ruby's voice was lost within her sobs. I didn't know who he was, but I remembered Ruby mentioning someone she met in college. A guy from Harlem with money. Was he the reason we hadn't spoken in so long? I lifted Ruby's face so she could look at me. She stared back at me through a black eye. Her bottom lip was swollen. I'd seen her like this before. When we played catch, Ruby would wince if the ball hit one of the bruises left by her father or stepmother.

"You can stay with me for however long you need to. Okay?"

Ruby nodded, and we slowly walked home.

Time moved both slowly and fast with Ruby. It was like a dream, our dream. This was the one we whispered to one another in the corners of our old church, or while sitting on the dock staring at the glittering lake. Veronica was away at an exchange program for a semester, so Ruby and I had the apartment all to ourselves. In the morning, Ruby cooked grits and fried eggs with homemade biscuits and jam. I painted by the window that overlooked the city, sipping my tea and reflecting on my night. The sweet scent of Ruby's neck and the curve in her lower back provided all the inspiration I needed for my art. I painted portraits of Ruby and made sculptures of our bodies. We floated around one another as young lovers do, but we could never keep our hands off one another for too long.

"You know I had planned on staying mad at you for way longer than I did." I lay with my head in Ruby's lap. She curled a strand of my hair in her hand.

"I know. I didn't mean to stop talking to you for so long. Life just got in the way. One minute I'm writing letters to you about college, and the next...I stopped."

"Because of him?"

"Maybe. But also, maybe because of me. Maybe because I was embarrassed."

I pushed up on one elbow to look at her. "About what?"

"I was still secretly upset you didn't come with me. And I wanted to make my life seem like it was amazing without you. In the beginning, it was. Everything was fun and exciting. But eventually, it wasn't. And there was nothing else I could say."

"You wanna tell me about him?"

"No. Let's change subjects. You think we could live like this forever?" Ruby asked.

"Of course not, it's a sin to be shackin' up before marriage."

Ruby playfully pushed my arm. I sat up in the bed until we were facing one another.

"Maybe we can. I mean people will probably always think we're roommates, but we'll know the truth," I said.

"You'll still want me even when I'm old and grey, with wrinkles all over?"

"I'm sure you'll be just as beautiful then as you are now. Besides, I'll be old and grey, with wrinkles all over too. So I doubt I'll have much of a choice."

Ruby flicked my thigh and lay back in the bed.

"I can see it now. Our life together. I'll be reading a book while you're painting. We'll be in a beautiful home and live simple lives."

"We'll have a garden?" I asked.

"Of course! And a kitchen where I cook French food like Julia Child's. I'll have an apron and pearls and everything."

"You've really thought about this."

"I have. In great detail. I even know that when I die, I don't want to have a funeral."

I looked at her. "Really? What's gonna happen to your body?"

"I want to be cremated. If I die first, I want you to scatter my ashes over the ocean, so I can come back as a whale."

"You have some strange daydreams, but I love that I'm in them with you."

We never talked about him again. I didn't even know his name, but he lingered between us. When we were at the bar, Ruby's eyes would gloss over and suddenly become distant amongst the heavy smoke and glitter. There were moments when she flinched if I moved a certain way. Ruby was there, but not all of her. Parts of her were with him. Parts of her would always be with him.

***

It had only been two months of our blissful reunion before there was a knock at our door. Ruby was on the couch reading a book. I was finishing up a painting for a client. The knock was soft at first but became faster, more frantic with the passing seconds.

"Coming!" I yelled, as I closed my robe and walked to the door. I opened it a crack.

"Can I help you?"

"Yeah, does Ruby live here?"

A book fell to the floor behind me and made clear who the stranger was. He was tall, with light brown skin and tiny freckles across his cheeks. He wore a suit, held a bouquet of flowers in his right hand, and smelled expensive. He looked our age, around seventeen or eighteen, but stood as if he were much older.

"And who's asking?"

"Her husband, George."

"Husband." I doubt he heard my whisper. Before I could close the door on his face, a hand touched my shoulder.

"It's okay. He can come in." Ruby looked at me with wide, apologetic eyes. All I could see was the bruise that had finally healed, as my mind replayed George saying husband like a bad reverb from the bar speakers. I stepped aside so George could walk in. His face lit up when he saw Ruby.

"Baby! I've missed you so much. I've been trying to reach you for months. I want you to come home."

"Why so my face can hit your fist again?"

His eyes shot to me as he shifted from side to side in his leather shoes.

"Don't look at her. She knows everything. My face would still look like a train wreck if it weren't for her."

He cleared his throat. "That won't happen again. I was going through some things, battling some demons. I've been working on myself. Cleaned my act up. I even brought you flowers and this." He handed Ruby the flowers and pulled a small jewelry box out of his pocket. To my surprise, there was a tiny, satisfied smile on Ruby's face as she took her gifts.

"You're married?" I asked.

Ruby's silence and lack of eye contact were all the confirmation I needed.

"Yes, she's married. What's it got to do with you?"

"More than you know, slim."

"Slim? You gotta problem with me or something, 'cause I don't even know who you are?"

It stung to hear him say he didn't know me. Had Ruby never mentioned her best friend, her first love, not even once?

"You don't have to know who I am. That black eye she came here with told me all I needed to know about what kinda man you are."

"Hey now, that's between me and her!"

"Then why did she come to me!"

Ruby hurried to stand between the two of us.

"Juliet! Can we talk alone?"

George leaned over to kiss Ruby on the cheek.

"I'll wait outside."

"Good idea," I muttered.

George sauntered out the door. Satisfied with what he knew was about to happen.

"Husband! Are you serious, Ruby?"

"I didn't know how to tell you."

"It's simple, hey Juliet you know the guy that gave me this fat lip was my husband."

"It wasn't easy to keep this from you."

"But you did it anyway. How long have you been married?"

"A year now."

"Wow, and I didn't get an invite to the wedding. Thought we were closer than that."

Ruby placed her hand on my arm. "You're my best friend. Of course I wanted to tell you. I just didn't know how, given our history."

"So are these past two months just a part of our history now? Because you're leaving with him, aren't you?"

Ruby remained silent, fidgeting with the bracelet George bought her.

"I know you don't understand. Maybe one day you will. But he's my husband. And he's good, really. He just has bad days."

"What happened to spending a lifetime together? What happened to growing old and wrinkly with one another?"

"I'm so sorry, Juliet."

George knocked on the door as a signal to Ruby. She quickly packed her one bag, and within a matter of minutes she was gone. Again.

I should've learned my lesson the first time. I should've known time with Ruby was too good to be true. I never liked moving on. I enjoyed holding onto things, people, objects, memories that made me feel safe in a constantly changing world. It took a month to return to my bar gig, and another to leave my apartment for more than just groceries and work. It took me two months to get rid of the art inspired by her and our time together. Toward the end of the fifth month, I made contact with the friends I'd made in the city and finally moved on from Ruby. When I was finally ready to rejoin the world, I wanted to do it big. My best friend, Tommy, invited me to a party. He came over at a quarter past nine to help do my makeup. His own face was gorgeously made up, and he was dressed to the nines.

"Why are you still in your robe with rollers in your hair?" he asked.

I sat on my bed, hunched over, staring at my closet.

"I don't know what to wear."

"Juliet honey, Ruby left, she's not dead. Heartbreak is hard as hell, but you have to keep going." Tommy handed me his floral handkerchief.

"Now wipe your face, sit up straight, and tell me what's the look for tonight. A classy Dorothy Dandridge in *Carmen Jones*, rest her soul? Or a look that's a little trashy, like a hooker in church?"

I sat up straighter and wiped my face.

"Definitely Dorothy. I need to feel gorgeous tonight."

"You're already there. Now please take that robe off and put this on." He handed me a red halter dress with a high slit. "With this dress, no one will be able to take their eyes off you. The best way to get over someone is to get under someone else."

I shimmied into the dress and sat down so Tommy could do my hair and makeup.

"So, you never officially told me what happened between you and Ruby."

"What's there to say? She came, she left, end of the story."

"I would believe that if you hadn't become a hermit all these months. I bet you haven't even been painting."

"I've been expressing myself through poetry lately. Maybe I'll become a Beat."

Tommy rolled his eyes. "You will not become a Beat. Your wardrobe is far too colorful for that. Now back to why you shut yourself off from the world."

"She's married, Tommy," I finally whispered.

"Like married, married?"

"Yes. Married, married."

"Shit."

"Shit indeed."

Tommy walked to the kitchen and returned with two glasses. "Drink this."

"What is it?"

"Whiskey."

I looked in the cup for a second. "I've always hated whiskey."

"That may be true, but tonight you need it. We're young and we're gorgeous. So, we're going to go out, dance the night away, flirt the night away, and forget all about those boring married people who have thrown their life away. Got it?"

"Got it."

"Now take a look."

I walked to the mirror and smiled at my reflection. "You've done it again. What would I do without you?"

"You would probably still have those rollers in your hair. Now let's go. Some night air will do you good."

Tommy and I hit all the usual bars and nightclubs. After a few hours of hopping around, we ended up at the party. Tommy's friend's house was smoky, and the lights were low. Couples danced in the corner. The house smelled of perfume, hairspray, and cigarettes. The conversations I heard ranged from politics to literature to what people ate for lunch. I'd missed being around people. I loved the heated conversations about what was going on in the world and making eye contact with someone cute across the room. My body yearned to move in unison with another body to the new hit song. After walking around the party for a few minutes, Tommy and I beelined to the dance floor. Tommy worked as a dancer too, and we knew how to draw attention. We fed off that energy, and it never took long for some brave individual to come up and ask one of us to dance.

A handsome young guy in a turtleneck and slacks approached Tommy. I didn't mind. I was too in the zone to care if I was dancing alone. After five months of grieving what could've been with Ruby, I needed to dance wildly without a care in the world, surrounded by strangers who were both loving and hating me. My body needed to release the memories and dreams of what was and what could've been. I kept dancing to the Supremes singing "You Keep Me Hangin' On" until I locked eyes with someone in front of me. He smiled a gapped-tooth smile and walked directly to me. Without missing a beat or uttering a single word, he joined my dance as if we'd done it a million times.

Someone put on "Yes, I'm Ready" by Barbara Mason, and everyone coupled up. Our eyes never left one another. He grabbed both of my hands and pulled me closer. I wrapped my arms around his neck as his hands moved to my waist. We swayed to the song, inches away from one another. "You gonna tell me your name, stranger?"

His smile widened at my assertive nature. "Roy. My name's Roy."

Chapter Seven

DESTINY TOOK ME TO her apartment without asking
questions. The only thing I've done here, for days, is rest. I
don't know why I couldn't walk into my house. It's my house
after all. Fortunately she didn't tell her mother I was over, or I
would've never gotten any peace. On my last day of resting,
Destiny reminds me about the party she invited me to with her
colorful friends.

"You don't have to go if you're not up to it," she says while
searching through her closet for her party outfit.

"Don't be silly. You invited me, so I'm going."

"Okay. My friend, Kat, is coming with us. She'll be over soon,
and she is dying to meet you."

"Why?"

"You're her idol."

***

I stare at myself in Destiny's mirror after a long hot shower.
When did my neck start to look so old? They say black doesn't
crack, but it sure can droop. My body's doing a lot of drooping.
Is this what my mother would've looked like if she had made it
to seventy-five? Shouldn't I be grateful that I did make it?
Aren't I one of the fortunate ones? I'm not so sure anymore.
The momentum of following through with my awakening plan
is beginning to wear off. I'm losing that excitement of going out
on my own and doing things I haven't done in years. I wonder if
it's even worth it, or if I'm too old. The lines that move across
my skin remind me of the ripples created by a pebble skipping
across a pond. Time is the pebble. My body is the water. The
lines start at my hands and move their way across the rest of my
body. My arms, breasts, neck, stomach, thighs, feet. The longer
I stare at the mirror, the more vulnerable I feel. Everything
about me is so visible. I have nothing to hide behind. I would've
hoped by now that hiding didn't have a place in my life, but it's

too familiar for me to remain unseen. Comfortable. Yet here I am, in a world that will never view my body as beautiful, desirable, or sexy, trying to convince myself that I am still all those things and more.

"There's no time for a pity party today, Juliet," I say to myself.

There's a knock at the bathroom door.

"Grandma, you all right in there?"

Am I all right? I've been asking myself that question all night.

"I'm fine honey, just getting ready."

"Okay. Once Kat gets here and you're done, we'll all head out."

"All right, I'll be out in a minute."

What am I doing going to a party full of twenty-somethings? I'm past the midlife crisis point, so I can't blame it on that. Maybe tonight I'll meet a young'un to dance with and have my own cougar story to tell during spades night at Lili's.

I trim my already short grey hair as carefully as if I were pruning my tomatoes. I repaint my nails with a new bottle of bright-red polish. My mother would call it the color of whores and sinners. I feel like a teenager headed to my first party, giddy with tingles that move throughout my entire body. My long, turquoise-beaded earrings look like the Caribbean Sea in the light. The heat hasn't let up since my birthday, so I use a book Destiny has in the bathroom to fan myself. It's barely doing the job.

I look through the small suitcase Destiny packed for me the night she picked me up. My clothes resemble a nun's closet. Boring, bland, grey, beige, black, and white. Every article of clothing in that bag reflects the perfect life I worked so hard to create. But I wasn't perfect, I was afraid. I continue to sift through my suitcase. I hope Destiny packed something with a little more life to it, something that screams I'm a seventy-five-year-old woman about to crash a party for infants. Destiny knocks on the bedroom door. I wrap a fluffy blue robe around my already warm body and open the door with a heavy heart. I should just come up with an excuse and tell Destiny I can't go out tonight. I'm sure she'll understand. I'm her grandmother. All it takes is one word about an aching part of my body, and I instantly receive the sympathy vote. Destiny pauses as she takes in my appearance.

"Grandma, why aren't you ready?"

This is my chance to send Destiny and her little friend on their way, pretend that I'm just a simple senior citizen who needs her rest, and make a beeline to my bed. I can forget all about my plan and return to the uneventful life I've created these past four years. My life can once more become predictable. There's only one problem. Destiny knows my awakening plan, and she would be more than happy to hold me accountable. I'm not in the mood to be chastised, so I let out an exasperated sigh and say, "I can't find anything to wear."

"That's okay. We can help you with that."

"Great," I mumble.

I look over at Destiny's friend, who hasn't taken her eyes off me since she walked through the door. She has a big, green, curly afro and freckles all over her medium-brown skin. Tattoos cover most of her body. She wears a short black skirt, black boots, and a fishnet top, and has one of the widest smiles I've ever seen. She looks cute as a button. Boy, I remember the days when I was as daring as she is right now. Tommy would've liked her. I give Destiny's friend a warm smile.

"Are you going to introduce your friend, Destiny?"

"Oh right, sorry. Grandma, this is Kat. Kat, this is Grandma."

I extend my hand. "I do have a name, child. You can call me Juliet. I was Juliet long before anyone ever called me Mom or Grandma."

"It's nice to meet you, Juliet, and can I just say that you are my idol."

"So I've heard. Now how is that possible? You just met me."

"You are out here living your truth in your seventies. To be open to exploring your sexuality at your age as a Black woman is so rare and taboo. My grandma would never talk to me about anything regarding her sexuality. It's like she has it tucked away in a neat little box hidden underneath her bed."

"Well, don't be too hard on your grandma. I was just like her at the beginning of this week. It's not so easy to explore your sexuality when there's no one to explore it with. And sometimes, it can feel like a relief to be past the point in your life where you have to worry about that type of stuff, even if you do have someone to share it with. Life isn't as simple as you may think." While Destiny pulls out clothing options for me to try on, Kat makes herself comfortable on the edge of the bed.

"You know what, you're so right, Juliet. I never thought of it that way."

"Of course not, the young don't have to think of the old, and they rarely do. Including myself when I was your age. The old, on the other hand, seem to constantly be reminded of the young."

"Maybe I should call my grandma. She lives all the way in Texas. I rarely see her."

"Maybe you should. Now that you know a little bit about me, tell me about yourself, Kat."

"Well, my pronouns are she/her, they/them. I use them interchangeably. I identify as pansexual, demisexual, a sacred prostitute, and in my spare time, I'm a sex worker."

"A sex worker you say. What does that entail?" I ask with the curiosity of a child.

"Mainly online webcam stuff. There are a lot of lonely, desperate, middle-aged men who enjoy being teased by women who could be their daughter's age. I've tried doing the whole stripper thing, but I have two left feet."

"Do you like it?" I ask.

"It's not bad. It pays the bills, and since my parents refuse to help pay for school and my apartment, I must do what I gotta do. I could easily be a manager at McDonald's while putting myself through school and making my parents proud in the process, but I'm a vegan. However, I do love to wear leather from time to time. When I do, I get more in tips than I would make in a week working at a fast-food chain."

"You know I used to do a little burlesque dancing myself."

Destiny pauses from outfit hunting. "Wait what? You've never mentioned that to me before."

"Oh yeah, back when I lived in San Francisco in the sixties. I was a dancer at this bar with a dear friend, Tommy. And you're right, it does pay the bills. Dancing at nightclubs helped me to pursue my art during the day. But I must admit I enjoyed all the attention I got dancing on that stage in nothing but lingerie. It was so freeing."

"You're grandma's a legend!" Kat whispers to Destiny.

Destiny stares at me as if she's seeing me for the first time. I think she's seeing Juliet and not her grandmother.

Destiny and I finally settle on a flowy, green-and-blue top and white bell-bottoms. Kat does my makeup and makes it a point to explain why one can never wear too much glitter. I beg to differ, and so does my face. We finally leave for the party at eleven fifteen. Kat and Destiny try to give me a quick gender and sexuality lesson during the twenty-minute drive. I'm taking mental notes. I wish I would've brought my notepad. There are so many terms, identities, things that I never knew existed. Luckily, I'm no stranger to the fluidity of sexuality, genders, and appearances. I am a part of the art world after all. I partied with drag queens in club basements and the backrooms of apartments before the queens became as popular as they are now. I dined with butch lesbians and painted portraits of men who knew they were far prettier than I was.

I can't figure out, during the lecture I'm receiving from Destiny and Kat, where I fit into their descriptions. Is there an identity for someone who waited until halfway through their seventies to fully come to terms with their sexuality? Confused. Hopeless perhaps. I keep listening as hard as I can, hoping something will call out to me. Nothing says, "Hey, this is who you are." Everything is flying over my head. Deep down, I always knew I was different. I was an outsider amongst my family and even amongst my friends in the art world. I was always hiding pieces of myself to not shake things up too much. I was even an outsider in my marriage. Roy was laid back and had a kind heart, but he was still a product of his time and stuck in his ways. He wouldn't have understood me. When we got married, I left behind the girl who had found freedom on those San Francisco streets. He wouldn't have known how to handle the fullest expression of a woman like that, a woman as free as white dandelion seeds blowing in the wind.

"You never gave me the chance to understand you."

I hear his voice whisper in my head. He's right. I didn't give him the chance. I was a coward instilled with the belief that the most important thing in the world was to find a good man and hold onto him for dear life, even if that meant hiding who I truly was.

Destiny's a horrible driver. We survive the bumps and swerves and finally arrive. The air smells of cotton-candy smoke and pot mixed with strong perfume and cologne. The parking lot is almost pitch black. If it weren't for the lights flashing from inside what appears to be an old warehouse, I wouldn't be able to see my own two hands in front of me. I follow Destiny and Kat, who walk to the line of people with ease and confidence. In most settings, I am overlooked, ignored, or nonexistent. Here at the party, at almost twelve in the morning, I am far from invisible. I have stepped into a new territory, and I can't tell if the group of staring eyes welcomes me or not. It takes everything within me to resist the urge to hold up my hands and say, I come in peace.

One by one, Destiny and Kat's friends introduce themselves in the same one-breath fashion as Kat did. Name, pronoun, gender, sexual orientation, repeat. Because of the quickness of their introductions, I can only remember that there's one guy, a person, another person, and another person who doesn't mind what they're called. I think I'm catching on pretty quickly.

"ID?"

A tall, muscular bouncer looks at me with all the seriousness in the world. I want to tell him to smile, not to take life so seriously. I don't think he'd take it well.

"Are you serious, Brian? You're really making her show you her ID? You know good and well she's over twenty-one. No offense, Grandma."

"None taken. And Destiny, tonight I'm Juliet, not Grandma." I show him my ID, feeling a little giddy for even being asked. It's been well over forty years since I've been carded. It's a rush I never knew I missed. As we finally make our way inside, I hear the people in line behind us whisper, "Who brought the grandma?"

The music is so loud it thuds in my head and body, and bounces my feet on the floor. My eyes follow the movement of the young people dancing. It's a little different from when I was their age, but not as different as some of my peers would like to believe. We did a whole lotta bumpin' and grindin', too, and would end up married and pregnant by the following year. Time may seem different, but humans stay relatively the same. There's the Goody Two-shoes, the raunchy, and folks who fall somewhere in between. It's like the spectrum Kat and Destiny were explaining to me in the car. I didn't quite get it then, but it's starting to make more sense as the night goes on.

What has changed over the years is the music. The kids in the club are skittering around like jumping beans to sounds and beats mixed by a DJ. Everything is high energy, contagious, and a bit overwhelming. I'm used to my quiet nights at home, not hanging out in clubs with half-naked people who leave trails of glitter as they stumble by me.

"Come on, Juliet, dance with me!" Kat grabs my hand and starts moving her body in a way that makes me want to call an ambulance. She looks like a snake surrendering to an earthquake, like earth surrendering to itself. She's in her natural element, free and wild. I close my eyes and move my body to the strange rhythm. I move slowly, from side to side, until my feet join in. I wonder if I too look like earth surrendering to itself, or if I just look like an old woman who needs to go to the hospital.

I was always a natural dancer. It doesn't take my body long to remember how to move alongside the music. I'm dancing in a hot, crowded club, surrounded by people of all different colors, genders, sexual orientations, and ages. My body feels like I'm flying, euphoric. Or like that time I dabbled in psychedelics when I was around Destiny's age. What would I have thought to dance alongside a seventy-five-year-old when I was young? Would I have gawked at the slow, intentional movements of the soft flesh before me? Would I advert my eyes because no one wants to be reminded of the road that lies ahead of them? It's too dark in the club to see the expression on people's faces as they observe the old woman in an unnatural habitat. I don't mind. Let them look. Let them soak in this aging body like a warm, soothing bath.

Every once in a while, I sneak glances at Destiny. She looks so much like Toni when she was younger. I have to stop myself from calling out, Toni! What are you doing here? I blink, and Toni's long, pressed hair is replaced by Destiny's short, curly tapered cut.

"Your grandma is so cool. I've never seen an older person move like that." I overhear Destiny's friend, Mandy, yell over the thumping music.

"Yeah, she is! And I've never seen her move like that until tonight."

"Is it strange?"

"To see her dance?"

"Yeah, and for her to be here with you in a club?" Mandy asks.

"Not strange, but definitely different."

"Well, for what it's worth, your grandma is hella cute."

"Ew, she's my grandma."

"I know, I'm just sayin' Grandma's single, I'm single, and I feel like she may be down to bake some cookies later on, ya know."

"Mandy you're not dating my grandma! But that doesn't mean someone else can't. Maybe I should make an online dating account for her."

"That would be cool. Make sure to share with me!"

"Not gonna happen."

I pretend I'm not listening when Destiny waves at me. An online dating account. Me, dating? The last person I went on a date with was Roy. What would I look like going on a date at my age? Don't start overthinking Juliet, just keep enjoying yourself.

I continue to soak in my moment of freedom, but I can feel the aches creeping into my body like a cat on the hunt for lunch. I've moved my body more in the past couple of hours than I have in the past couple of years. If I keep going at this pace, I will be paying a heavy price in the days to come.

"I'm gonna take a seat, Kat."

"I'll come with you."

"Oh no, sweetie, you stay. I can see all that energy wanting to burst out of you. You keep dancing. When you have a minute, look to your right, because someone has been eyeing you for quite some time."

Kat turns to her right and spots one of her friends, who quickly averts his gaze when their eyes meet.

"Who, Kevin?"

"If that's his name, then yes."

Kat takes another look at him and tilts her head to the side like a puppy waiting for a treat. "Kat and Kevin. I think it has a good ring to it."

"As do I. Now go on and ask him to dance."

"Me, go ask him to dance?"

"Yes, why not? This is the twenty-first century. If you truly are as liberated as you appear to be, then you should have no problem."

"You know what, you're right, Juliet. If I leave it up to that boy, he may never ask me to dance. I'm sure you didn't have to worry about that in your day. Now people only know how to like one another if they're pressing a heart or thumbs up button on their phones."

"We had our problems back then. Now go on girl, you're wasting time talkin' with me."

Kat skips off and immediately pulls Kevin to the dance floor. He looks terrified, but after the shock leaves his body, they start dancing wildly in a way that only young folks with no worries and strong bones could.

I finally take a seat in a booth off to the side. Watching the young people dancing in front of me is like watching the birds from my front porch. The young folks are in their zone, and the rest of the world has disappeared. People who call the young reckless have forgotten how they once felt as worry-free as the birds. As much as I'm enjoying myself, I know for a fact I don't want to be young. I had my time being young, dumb, and wild. I've been where they are and where they're trying to go. I'm enjoying myself, but this type of club is for twenty-something Juliet, not for seventy-five-year-old Juliet. And I'm perfectly fine with that.

"You know you have to go home, right?" I turn to look at Roy, sitting next to me in the booth tapping his foot to the beat. The neon lights dance against his white hair.

"There's nothing for me there."

"Are you kidding, woman? Your whole life is there."

"My whole life is not in that house."

He looks at me. "Is it not?"

"No, it's not."

"You can't stay with Destiny forever. I don't know what's gotten into you. When you said you needed to start living again, I thought you meant going out more, being independent again. Not parading around town like you're a teenager."

"I might as well parade around town. I feel just as lost as a teenager! And I've never been fully independent, not for long anyway. I went from growing up in my mother's house to taking care of her. I got a tiny glimpse of freedom before marrying you and taking care of Toni. I took care of my father, then you. Where has all that gotten me?" I look around at the young faces passing by me. They have so much life to live, so much time and space.

"I've taken care of everyone else for so long I forgot how to take care of myself. I've been running on autopilot. Now it's just me. Just me."

I wave Destiny over to my booth. "Are you enjoying yourself, Juliet?" Destiny's smile is just like Roy's.

"I am. So much so that it's time for me to leave."

"What? No you can't go. The night's still young."

"Yes, but I am not." I pat her hand. "This has been one of the most exciting nights I've had in a while. Thank you for inviting me. Now you go on back out there and have fun."

"Okay well, I'll see you back at home."

I shake my head. "No dear, it's time for me to go home to my home. I'll see you when you come over."

"Okay Grandma, I mean Juliet. I'll text you when I get home."

"Tell everyone I said it was nice meeting them." As I walk out of the nightclub all I can think of is how nice my bed is going to feel after a long, hot shower.

***

My bed never felt as good as it does right now. The window is cracked to let in the cool, late-summer-night air. I'm not wearing my usual pajamas. The last time I slept in my bed with no clothes on was when Roy was alive and still strong enough to make love. It's been five years, maybe six. My ears are still ringing from the club's music, and the pores in my skin are vibrating from all the high energy that circulated in me throughout the night. I could never sleep well after coming back from an event. But I try to relax as much as possible, because sleep is all I want to do, and deeply at that.

As the night air blows on my bare back and neck, I feel a tingling sensation between my thighs. I push back the covers to make sure nothing was crawling on me in my honey pot. If something is crawling on me, that's what I get for suddenly wanting to be naked all the time. Nothing's there. I settle back into my bed and have the strangest urge to whisper to her, Well hello, old friend, it's been a minute.

I decide against it. Mainly because a tiny part of me thinks if I speak, I'll spook her. I close my eyes and allow myself to feel. The tingling sensation moves up and down my body. My toes slightly curl, and the tiniest moan I've ever made escapes my mouth. Images of both Roy and Ruby lying in bed with me pop into my mind. I ride the sensation for as long as I can, until it fades and my body becomes heavy with sleep.

Chapter Eight

I'VE BEEN SPLITTING MY life in two. One where I'm mom, wife, daughter, and the other where I'm just Juliet. I've forgotten my name many times. I spent long, sleepless nights with a teething eight-month-old. I was so caught up in making sure Roy was receiving pleasure and that I was putting on a good show, I forgot the person he was making love to should also experience pleasure. I was dutiful. I disappeared and reappeared as if nothing ever happened, as if I hadn't forgotten Juliet. I pretended I was there all along, but I wasn't. When I looked in that mirror on my birthday and danced until my body felt like it was floating, I knew that Juliet, the free one, had been gone for a long time.

I feel like I was hit by a truck. I didn't drink, yet I think I have a hangover. At least I can feel it. I can feel the cracks in my bones, the dull ache in my lower back, and the stiffness in my toes. At least I feel something.

No wonder my body is protesting this morning. She's gotten so used to her routine that she knows when something is off. I suppose something is off, but I'm happy I went. I don't know what time I got back, but I made sure to text Destiny. I let her know my first time going out to one of her clubs would be my last. I don't need to hang around young people to make me feel alive. Being alive doesn't have to do with age. It has to do with living. Twenty-somethings only know how to live in a twenty-year-old world. Most of my twenties were a hot mess. I didn't know if I was coming or going. There were times I wished I could give it all back, the husband and child, and just be an artist. I used to imagine living in the tiniest Parisian apartment, painting as the rain trickled down my windows. I would go to all the parties of the other Black artists who moved to the City of Lights in hopes of being seen as more than their skin complexion. I would smoke socially and wear clothing that made people say, Oui, that woman is a true artist. I would've had multiple lovers, both men and women. Perhaps I'd have been a mistress to a wealthy man who was great in bed but horrible at everything else.

Then there were other times when I wished I was never an artist. I spent my days as a full-time mother and wife, a homemaker. I would wake up in the morning and cook a big breakfast. I'd comb my daughter's hair and kiss my husband before he headed to work. I did the laundry and played with the child, all in a flowy dress and apron that, of course, I sewed myself. I would hum softly throughout the day. When Roy returned home from work, I had his dinner ready. I bathed Toni and put her to sleep, then made love to Roy. I had to sleep pretty—not allowing Roy to see my hair messed up—and wake the next morning to do it all over again.

These were the thoughts that filled my twenties, trying to figure out my place in the world. I don't miss it. I don't envy any of them.

I walk through my house in the morning light, going to every room and really looking at it. I move with slow, intentional footsteps. My house is smaller than I remember. Darker and more closed in. I still have furniture from when Toni was a child, and the floral wallpaper hasn't changed since Roy and I first moved into this house. I've always been gifted art from friends all over the world. I kept them in my painting room, hidden from Toni, who was prone to breaking everything. My house is not mine at all. I've meticulously curated every room to be perfect for everyone except me. I walk into my art room and drag out three big buckets of yellow paint. I bought it for a mural project I was thinking of doing but never got around to. That paint is meant for more than a mural. My body aches from last night's dancing, but I need something in this house to be mine, even if it's just a yellow wall.

A day passes, hours of painting over the white floral wallpaper in the living room. By the time the sun replaces the moon, I'm fast asleep on the couch, happily exhausted. If it weren't for the doorbell, I would still be asleep. I look at the clock on my wall. It's eleven in the morning. I'm usually up with the birds, but it sure felt good to sleep in. My back and hips are punishing me. I stretch out my arms and am met with a chorus of cracking bones. It takes me a minute to remember how I got on the sofa in the first place.

Then I see it. It's as yellow as the sun. My wall.

I finally open the door.

"Thank goodness you're okay, Grandma." Destiny flings her arms around me, and Kat matches her hug. "We thought something had happened to you when you didn't answer the phone."

I squeeze their hands. "I'm fine. I just got caught up in redecorating, that's all." They walk in and look at all the yellow paint cans, piles of artwork, and furniture pieces piled into corners.

"It looks like you're doing a little more than redecorating. I don't think I've ever seen your house change." Destiny is looking through my art pieces.

"That's because it hasn't."

"Well, do you need any help? We have time. And after you helped me with Kevin last night, I'm definitely down to grab a paintbrush." Kat reaches for a paint can.

Having them help me would make it easier and quicker, but I want to do this on my own. I know there's a possibility I will never see it completed at the rate I'm going, but is that not life? Doing things in the hope of seeing it to the end, but never truly knowing if that will happen or not.

"I'm okay. I'm just taking things slow. And just ask Destiny. I'm very particular."

"Extremely particular," Destiny confirms

"So what brought you two by besides checking on me?"

Destiny plops onto the couch and grabs my hand to pull me down next to her.

"Actually, we have some exciting news."

My heart speeds up. Could they have found Ruby so soon? "Well, go on. I'm too old to be kept waiting for so long."

"We signed you up for online dating!" Destiny says with a toothy smile.

"Come again?"

"Online dating!" Kat says louder and slower.

"Sweetie, I can hear. But isn't online dating for people your age?"

Destiny whips out her laptop from her backpack and pulls up the dating website. "Oh no. There's online dating for basically everyone. This particular website is tailored to people fifty and above. It's really cool. All you do is see who's a match, chat for a little bit, set up a date, and go from there."

"I don't know, Destiny. I don't think I'm ready to start dating again."

Destiny grabs my hand. "I never told you this, but before Grandad passed, he made me promise to make sure that you're not alone for too long. That was him giving his blessing. Not to mention, this goes perfectly with your awakening plan. You wanted adventures and more opportunities to go out. Well here you go. Nothing is stopping you right now but you. You asked me to help you with your sexuality. I think this is a great place to start."

Destiny knows her points are solid, and she can already see the wheel of acceptance spinning in my head.

"Okay fine. But it's been a long time since I've had suitors knocking on my door. It may take a while for me to get some matches on that website."

"Are you kidding, Ms. Juliet! You're a hit. We made this profile last night, and you already have twenty matches," Kat says.

"Twenty people want to take me out on a date. That's more people than I've ever dated in my entire life."

I stare at all the faces lined up next to mine on the computer screen. Stranger after stranger has found something that attracted them to me. It makes me squirm a bit in my seat.

"Oh and, Ms. Juliet, I thought of the perfect way to thank you for helping me out with Kevin. My favorite aunt just moved to town. She's like seventy or maybe sixty-eight, I don't know, but she's like a serious OG lesbian. And I think you two would be adorable together. I told her about you, and she agreed to meet you for coffee. I told her I would ask you if it's okay. Please say yes, please say yes!"

I'm trying to fully comprehend everything that just came out of Kat's mouth. The girl can talk faster than a hamster running on a wheel. Did I hear her right? Adorable together... I haven't been out on a date in over fifty years. I don't even know what to do on a date in this day and age. And on top of that, a date with a woman. What is an OG lesbian? No doubt it's someone who knows who they are and who has known for quite some time. She'll take one look at me and see I'm a fraud. Yes, I've researched online about my sexuality. Yes, the quizzes say I am somewhere along the lines of something known as queer. And yes, my first love was Ruby. But that was ages ago. Am I ready to share something I've kept buried and hidden from the world for so many years? Everything's moving faster than I thought it would.

"Grandma, are you okay? You're looking a little flush. I'll bring you some water." Destiny hops up to grab a glass of water from the kitchen as I watch the yellow paint dry.

"I think I may have dropped that load on you too fast. I do that a lot. Sometimes I just start talking and it's really hard for me to stop. My mom says it comes from a good place, but…"

I place my hand on Kat's knee.

"I just need a minute, that's all."

Kat nods. "Noted. Do you mind if I look around your art space?"

"Go for it." I welcome the silence. Destiny returns, glass in hand. The water sliding down my throat feels like a baptism.

"Sorry about Kat. I told her she couldn't just pimp my grandma out. Although I guess I kinda did the same thing with the online dating profile. We shouldn't have crossed the line like that without checking with you first."

I laugh softly to myself at the thought of being pimped out. According to my mother, the prize life offered to those born a girl was to find a husband who would take care of them. I once believed my mother was so committed to this mission that she went as far as making sure she fell ill right as I was about to run off with Ruby. In a way, I feel as if I've been pimped out to the world since I was a child.

It's been years since I've thought of myself as desirable. I was always taught the honorable thing to do is to retire feelings like desire and save them for the young. The older athlete has already proved themselves to the world and passes a torch to the younger, shinier athlete more than eager to replace them. I was brainwashed by a society obsessed with youth. Without a fight, I gave up being someone worthy of love, desire, affection. But that doesn't explain the tingling between my thighs the other night. It doesn't explain the flutters in my stomach when I think about the possibility of going on a date. Whoever says pleasure is reserved strictly for the young—excuse my language—but fuck that and fuck them!

"Kat!" I call out.

Kat, who is staring at my paintings in awe, whips her head around to look at me. "Yes?"

"Tell your aunt I would like to meet her for coffee or tea. And Destiny, set me up on one of those dates."

"Grandma, are you sure?"

Am I sure?

"I'm not sure of anything in my life anymore, but I said I wanted to live more adventurously. What better way to do that than with a little romancing." The birds outside the front window burst into a chorus of confirmations. It's a sign. Birds always know the right moments to sing. And I'm slowly learning the right moments to say yes.

Chapter Nine

ROY WAS ONE OF the most arrogant guys I had ever met. He thought flashing his smile and winking his eye was enough to make me walk down the aisle. So what, he was a good dancer. So he smelled like fresh strawberries in spring. I wasn't those other girls in the city. I didn't need to chase after him. He could chase after me.

Tommy and I had found an apartment together. I was cooking dinner, and Tommy was lounging on the sofa, fiddling with an old camera he'd found.

"So, are you going to call him?" Tommy asked

"Now, why would I do that? I'm dating a professor."

"Because he is finer than wine and not some creepy old man dating a student."

"I'm not his student."

"You might as well be. Come on, Juliet. I get it. Your professor guy is gorgeous, but you two don't have the spark like you and Roy."

"I met Roy once. We danced once. He doesn't even know my name. There was no spark."

"I beg to differ. If there weren't a spark, I'm sure he wouldn't be asking all around the city for you. Besides, if you don't date him, I will."

"I don't think you're his type."

"Maybe. Maybe not. But *you* are. From what I've heard, he doesn't ask girls on dates often. No matter how much they may want him to."

"So what, I should be honored? I don't have time for dating right now. I'm just having fun with the professor. Mostly, I'm focusing on my art. There's a new gallery opening, and I'm hoping they'll sell some of my paintings."

"All work and no play is seriously no fun. Besides I know this is about the one who shall not be named. But you can't let one breakup stop you from love."

"I'm not the Supremes. Love's got nothing to do with me right now."

Tommy grabbed my hand and took me to the mirror.

"Do you see that girl staring back at you? She is one of the most courageous girls I've ever met, and she deserves all the love that comes her way."

"But what if it ends in another heartbreak?"

"Easy, you just get some glue to mend your heart and begin again. Now let's get ready for your boring professor's party. I'm sure I'll need a nap."

***

We walked into a room filled with academics of all types. "Who knew nerds like to party," Tommy whispered.

"Be nice," I whispered back.

We circled the group, attempting to make small talk. This was not like our vibrant parties. The professor kept me by his side, as he went around talking to his friends and colleagues. He enjoyed having a pretty, young woman on his arm. I was his shiny new trophy, and he was making sure to show me off. I walked over to grab a drink, happy to be away from him for a second. I felt as if I couldn't breathe. If another person asked me about my opinion on the war in Vietnam or the Department of Defense communication satellites being launched, I was going to scream.

"You know, I knew we would meet again." Roy was checking me out, with his hands in his pockets and a half smile on his face. "You just couldn't get enough, could ya?"

"Your arrogance may work on other girls but not me."

"Oh I see, 'cause you're not like other girls. No, you date professors twice your age. You like distinguished men."

"Better than boys. Yes."

"The way we were dancing the other night, we were neither a boy nor a girl. Just two bodies creating magic."

"How did you even know I would be here?"

Roy grabbed a grape off the fruit platter and popped it in his mouth. "I didn't. My cousin is a student of one of these bow tie-wearin' types. He invited me. I had nothing else to do. So I came."

"Is that right?"

"Yeah, that's right. So you gonna finally tell me your name?"

The professor held up his glass to get everyone's attention. "Juliet!" The professor called out as he waved me over. Before I walked away to join him, I turned to look back at Roy. "Now you know."

The night went by in a boring blur. Tommy, of course, found someone to go home with. The professor invited me to go to a diner with some of his friends. I graciously but quickly declined. I said my goodbyes and happily left the party. It was a nice night to walk home. The breeze from the ocean helped to wake me up after the dull evening. Before I'd walked too far down the block, I heard my name.

"Hey, Juliet!"

Roy was walking toward me. I could have told him to leave me alone or ignored him and kept walking. But I heard Tommy's words in my head. I didn't believe Roy and I would fall in love, but I was tired of being shown off like a prized poodle. I was ready to have some fun.

When he was inches away from me, he paused and smiled down at me. "You headed anywhere in particular?"

"Not really, just walking. Enjoying the night air."

"Can I join you?"

I thought about it. This night could've been worse. I could've been discussing current events with a bunch of bow tie-wearin' types.

"Maybe. Under one condition."

"What's that?"

"The night only ends when I say it does."

"Easy. I can do that. Anything else?"

"Well, after that boring jam, I need to have some fun. I didn't get all dolled up just to go home early."

"Say no more." He held out his hand. "Can I take you to one of my favorite spots in the city?"

Without thinking twice, I took his hand and nodded. His hand was warm and a little rough. There wasn't an electric spark like they talked about in movies. When my hand pressed against his, I felt safe. And not like a backup plan kind of safe, but a home kind of safe. I'd never felt that kind of safe with anyone except Ruby.

"Can we get some food first? I'm starving." My audible stomach rumbles proved the point.

"Hey this is your night. I'm just along for the ride."

We walked to a diner a few blocks away. I ordered a burger, fries, strawberry milkshake, and apple pie. I was always taught not to eat in front of a man, especially on a first date. But I didn't consider this a date, and I hadn't eaten anything since breakfast. I ate almost religiously. Roy sat across from me with a toothpick in the side of his mouth. He fidgeted with the root beer bottle cap in front of him and never took his eyes off me.

"Aren't you gonna eat something, instead sittin' there staring at me?"

He laughed. "I think you may be eatin' for the both of us."

"Ha, ha not funny. What am I supposed to be eating, a salad?"

"Most girls do. Especially you artist types."

"Well maybe you shouldn't lump us all together."

"Maybe I shouldn't. You're not from this city, are you?"

I popped a fry in my mouth. "Nope."

"Where you from?"

"Georgia. Know of it?"

"I think I may have heard about it once or twice." He smiled and took a swig of his root beer.

"Are you from here?"

"No, I'm from Ohio. Cleveland actually."

"What brought you out here?"

"My cousin had a job for me, and I needed a change of scenery and a little more sunshine. No better place than California, right?"

I shrugged. "I guess. Georgia gets more sunshine than here."

"Then why did you come?"

I took a sip of my milkshake and looked out the window at people walking past, enjoying the city's nightlife. "Freedom. I wanna be like the birds you know."

Roy sat back in his seat and took the toothpick out of his mouth. "Freedom from what exactly?"

"Not a freedom from something, but a freedom to do and be whatever makes my soul sing."

"I can dig that. I think a lot of us who came out here are lookin' for something similar."

"Yeah, I think so too."

I dropped my cloth napkin onto my plate. "Now that I've been fed, I'm ready for some fun. Where are we going, a groovy underground club, a blues joint, a jam where we can dance all night?"

"You'll see. And you'll love it. Promise."

I grabbed my purse and walked to the door. "Don't make promises you can't keep now."

He laughed. "Noted."

We walked along the city streets, passing Victorian houses with young people gathered on the front steps. San Francisco was always so fascinating at night, the complete opposite of my small hometown where most things closed by the time the sun set. Roy reached for my hand. My first instinct was to pull back. What if someone I knew saw us walking around together? What if, somehow, word got back to Ruby that I was walking around the city at night, holding the hand of another? Oh, what the hell. We weren't walking down the aisle. We walked through Chinatown holding hands. Bright neon lights in Chinese characters hung beside swaying lanterns, and chubby Buddhas sat on display in windows. Unfamiliar music drifted out from shops and clubs. People sold food and knickknacks from their stalls. The scent of foods I had never smelled before lingered as we walked past restaurants.

"It's like we're in a whole new world," I said with awe.

"It's one of my favorite spots in the whole city."

"You know I've never been here. I remember seeing it on the news back home but never got around to coming. It's incredible."

"Let me show you this one spot. I'm sure you'll love it."

He took me to a music bar with a woman wearing the most beautiful dress I had ever seen. He told me the dress was called *Hanfu*. She looked like a watercolor painting come to life. We sat at a table in the back by the bar. My eyes were glued to the stage, where she sang and danced.

"She's beautiful."

"Yeah." Out of the corner of my eye I could see that Roy's eyes were glued to me. My cheeks grew warm under his gaze.

"So is this the favorite spot you wanted to take me to?" I wanted to change the subject and hoped he hadn't noticed me blushing.

"It's one of them, but actually, it's on the way to my favorite spot."

"Well, what if I wanted to end the date right now?"

Roy smiled. "This is a date?"

"Night. I meant night." My cheeks were on fire. I needed to get a grip.

"Well, I wouldn't let you end the *night* right now."

"You wouldn't be able to stop me."

"No, I'm sure I wouldn't. But whether you admit it or not you're having a good time, better than the night you were having with that stuffy professor. And I don't think you would leave before knowing how it's going to end."

"Then where to next?"

We left the performance and continued walking through the busy streets. I pointed to a Ferris wheel in front of us. "Let's go on that!"

"You sure?"

"Yeah, I've always wanted to go on one. Now's the chance."

We rode the Ferris wheel, watching the city grow and shrink around us.

"I love this city. I'm never going back home if I don't have to."

"Yeah, I love this city, too, from the ground."

For the first time, Roy didn't look like his usual nonchalant self. His hands were gripping the rail in front of us, and he was barely keeping his eyes open. I had to admit he *was* really handsome with his high cheekbones and almond-shaped brown eyes. I placed my hand on top of his. His eyes opened and met mine.

"You afraid of heights?"

"What gave me away?"

"Your death grip on that rail for starters. Why didn't you just say so, tough guy?"

"You looked so excited. I can push my fear to the side for a short while to see you smile like that."

Maybe it was the Ferris wheel that was making my stomach flip or maybe it was the way Roy looked at me. Whatever it was, I hadn't felt it since Ruby left. It was both frightening and exciting, and I wasn't ready for the night to end. Not even close.

We left Chinatown and made our way to the outskirts of the city. The streets grew darker as we moved farther away from the city lights.

"You sure you know where you're going?" I was rethinking my decision to follow a practical stranger simply because he was cute.

"Of course, I come here all the time. We're not far."

We walked up to a large junkyard. Roy helped me squeeze through an opening in the fence. Besides the stars above us, it was pitch black. I held on tightly to his hand, sure I would trip over a car part. Finally, we made it to the middle of a wide-open baseball field.

"You brought me to a baseball field?" I looked around at the empty stands. Roy ran off to the side and pulled out a bat and baseball.

"It's my favorite place to come to outside the city. Ever played?"

"Sure, I used to play softball back home. But just for fun."

"Good. Then you should know the rules."

"I am not playing baseball in these heels and in this dress."

"Hey, it's okay if you're not that good. Your secret will be safe with me."

"Oh, I'm good."

He returned to his usual arrogant demeanor. "Prove it."

I kicked off my heels and pulled my dress up until it was around my thighs. Roy's eyes widened and he quickly averted his gaze.

I smiled, as I walked over and grabbed the ball out of his hand. "Now I'm ready. Come on."

We made up our own rules. The game consisted of a lot of laughter, a lot of trash talk, and a ton of touching. By the end of the game, we were lying on our backs in the middle of the field, sweaty and out of breath.

"You ever think about the future? Like where you'll end up?" Roy asked.

"All the time. Sometimes too much."

"What do you think about, your dream wedding and perfect family?"

I scoffed. "Please, I'm not getting married. And I don't think about having kids. I think about traveling the world and living in exotic places as an artist."

"Why don't you want to get married?"

"People lose themselves once they get married. I don't wanna lose myself."

"I guess that can happen. But sometimes people find themselves in a marriage. For what it's worth, I think you'll make an amazing wife and mother to someone, if you choose to."

I tucked a piece of loose hair behind my ear. "What about you? What do you think about?"

"I think about being a good husband and father, living in a nice house, and growing old with the people I love around me."

I turned over on my side to look at him. "Sounds nice. I hope you get that one day."

He turned to face me. "I'm sure I will."

Our bodies inched closer together until my lips were pressed against his and our arms wrapped around one another. He pulled back. "You ready to end the night?"

"Not even close."

"Would you consider this a date now?"

"Just shut up and keep kissing me."

Chapter Ten

I DON'T WANT TO age gracefully. I want to age like a wild woman with jagged teeth and claws. I don't want to be the nice little house granny knitting sweaters that no one wants to wear. I want to slip off into the woods and befriend a coyote. I want these seventy-five-year-old legs to not only stop traffic but to stop the fiercest of bears in its tracks. I want to keep my hands in the dirt and have children whisper, Is she a witch? as they pass by my cabin. I don't want to be feared, but I also don't care about being understood. At one time, all I wanted was to be understood, to be seen. I wanted to fill my time with noise and people and life experiences. Why did I stop saying yes? We're taught, as women, as folks with brown skin, never to be too eager. We don't want to scare off life, men, and the possibility of a happy future. We're supposed to keep our heads down and graciously decline opportunities that come our way out of fear disguised as humbleness. That fear is etched into our life's map, reminding us we are not deserving of all the good in life. My mother used to say we are meant to be the lamb. But I've been the sacrificial lamb far too long. I must say that I'd much rather be an elephant. Big and wide and loud, demanding to be seen. I deserve these upcoming dates. My old friend Tommy, whose wisdom I last heard before his death at the age of thirty, said I deserve love. I deserve a home that feels like a sanctuary of peace when I walk in through the door. I deserve to have a little fun.

I recall visiting a friend's family in Japan. They were poor in terms of money, but they had the most beautiful garden I had ever seen. Their traditional home was built by the hands of an ancestor. There was beauty in the teaware, the lines of the furniture, and in the empty spaces. Everything in their home had a purpose. That's what I want. A home that is artful, purposeful...and empty.

I'm clearing everything besides necessary furniture from my home and creating my very own private oasis. I've been painting walls, one by one, with the attention and enthusiasm of an artist.

The old lamp belonged to my mother. Every time I look at it, a wave of shame washes over me, and I hear my mother's voice pointing out every incorrect thing in my life. It's easy to give away that lamp. Roy and I bought the coffee table together when we first moved in here. This one is much harder to let go of. I watch the young couple load the table into the back of their pickup truck and feel as if a piece of my heart has been tugged from my chest and strapped on for the ride. With each item I give away, I become less attached. The coffee table sat in a corner collecting dust and old magazines for years. I don't need it, and it's not Roy. Junk. It's just junk.

After weeks of getting rid of so much stuff, my house resembles a Zen Buddhist temple. Finally, I can breathe. My walls are sparsely decorated with paintings and sculptures. I painted each room a different color. The living/dining room is a soft yellow. The kitchen is mint green. My bedroom is now a burnt orange, and my bathroom went from beige to dusty rose. My home smells of fresh bundles of lavender that are hanging to dry in my kitchen. There's newly stacked wood beside my fireplace from one of my neighbors, in preparation for the cool fall weather. The kitchen table is covered with seeds I collected from my garden this morning, and the porch is covered with one of my favorite things, fallen red and yellow leaves. My house is as colorful and vibrant as I feel on the inside. This is the home of an artist. I no longer have to hide within the four walls of my art room. I can glide throughout my house like a lost swan returning to its sparkling blue lake after a long journey.

***

I decide to take myself on another date. One of my favorite multi-media artists, Sydney, is giving a lecture on her new collection. It's the perfect date to feed my stifled, inner artist. Sydney's brilliant, spunky, and the exact opposite of how I was when I gave lectures on my art. I never enjoyed standing in front of an audience at a local college, giving a speech about my paintings, my process as an artist, and what it took to become a renowned painter. It was always the same. My story isn't

75

unique. I didn't go to college. My parents were not artists. I didn't struggle my way through life, painting day in and day out, to become known and respected. If success happened it happened, if it didn't it didn't. I painted because it was the only thing I could truly call my own.

"What was the moment when everything took off for your art career?" The young woman with short, red locs and circular, gold-frame glasses in the front row has a notepad, ready to jot down whatever she finds inspiring. There's always someone like her in the audience. Someone hoping they will hear the one thing that will point them in the right direction to reach their desired outcome. I smile at the young woman, remembering how I was once searching for the answers to life—actually I'm still searching for the answers.

"The moment when everything took off is hard to pinpoint. I believe there were many little moments."

I glance around the room as Sydney explains her journey as an artist. Everyone's hooked, except for a woman sitting in the back who looks to be around my age. I catch her staring at me more than once. Do I know her? I try to be inconspicuous by pretending to drop my pen to get a better look, but I end up drawing more attention to myself.

"Ladies and gentlemen, I cannot end this lecture without acknowledging one of my favorite artists, who has deeply inspired my work. Juliet Livingston is here with us today." The clapping audience turns toward me, as I awkwardly pick up my pen.

I stand and give a small wave.

The woman sitting in the back raises her hand, and Sydney motions permission to ask her question. "I have a question for Juliet." I turn to meet her gaze. What question does she have for me?

"Are you planning on returning to the art world anytime soon? We've missed your work."

"I second that question!" Sydney chimes in.

"Well, I appreciate being missed. I don't feel as if I ever truly left. But if you're asking when the art world will see another one of my paintings, I do not know. Perhaps soon."

The talk ends with the signing of Sydney's new book. I walk outside with my copy and take in the refreshing evening air. The older woman who asked the last question walks out moments later and lingers beside me. Okay, now this is getting strange. I turn to face her, but before I can get a word out, her hand is already extended toward me.

"I know you probably think I'm acting a little odd. I'm Elena. I'm just so surprised to see you here."

I cautiously take her hand. "Juliet. I'm sorry, do we know each other? My memory is failing me right now."

"No, your memory is probably perfectly fine. I'm the one who should explain myself. I'm Kat's aunt and your date for tomorrow."

I almost drop my book. My mind has been so wrapped up in redoing my house and planning all of the dates I'm taking myself on that I entirely forgot about the first blind date I'm supposed to go on tomorrow. I fully look at Elena for the first time. Thick, white curls nearly reach her belly and contrast with her dark, olive skin. She appears to be the OG lesbian her niece proclaimed. I smile inwardly at the combined scents of coffee, flowers, and the backstage of a reggae concert. Pungent, sweet, and earthy. Stained teeth further confirm her habits. She's short, and her hazel eyes are bright with life. Her green corduroy jacket and jeans fit loosely around her small frame. She's charming. I'm sure she pulled many heartstrings in her day, and probably pulls even more now that she's older.

She waits patiently for my response, as if she has nowhere else to be but right in front of me. What do I say? What if I respond in the coy manner I used to in my younger years? I'd say something like, What on earth would we be doing on this date you just have to take me on?

They'd blush and I'd bat my long eyelashes, sneaking glances to show I was interested but not too desperate. Or maybe I should take the opposite approach and project any insecurities I may have about dating again at my age. Are you sure you're talking about the right person? I'm sure there's some twenty-year-old, budding lesbian prancing around here who would just love someone to take care of her and show her the ways of the world. Maybe she's the one you're going on a date with.

I decide not to play coy or insecure, and say the only thing I can think of, "Thank you. I look forward to our date tomorrow."

"As do I. Do you know the little café by the bookshop in town?"

I smile. "Café Daisy? Yes, I know it."

"How about we meet there for breakfast, say around ten?"

"Sounds like a plan."

Elena's eyes seem kind, as she nods her head forward slightly, then walks away. What did I just get myself into?

Chapter Eleven

I'M WOKEN BY THE rumble of the garbage truck driving down the street. I can't believe it. I have a date with a woman I just met yesterday. And apparently, according to Destiny, I have another date with someone else the day after. I can't stop thinking about what my dates will be like. They'll probably be obnoxious, or maybe they're going on the date to win a bet. What if I spend the entire date thinking about the fact that they're not Roy? But there was a life before Roy. There was a time when it was Ruby's hand I held. And there's a life after Roy. If the roles were reversed and I watched him from wherever spirits go, I would be highly upset if he were living the life I have been living. My heart isn't dried up yet. Maybe I'm ready to give it to someone again.

***

I want to feel sexy, but I don't want to appear as if I'm trying too hard. So I settle on a denim maxi skirt and knee-high boots, because nothing screams seductive like knee high boots. To tie the outfit together, I pair the skirt and boots with a forest-green turtleneck and multicolored, quilted coat. Although I'm embodying my inner Pam Grier with this outfit, I'm still nervous. I find my keys in one of the kitchen drawers and head out into the crisp morning air. The smell of fresh bread from the bakery up the road floats in the air. I would walk if I had more time, but I'm almost late. In the car, I do some breathing techniques I learned in a yoga class. I never liked bending my body in ways that resemble branches of a tree, but I developed a severe case of anxiety in my fifties while taking care of my sick father. The breathing exercises were the only thing that helped. By the time I arrive at the café, my nerves are finally settled.

I walk behind a woman in her twenties or thirties in yoga pants and a long, straight ponytail. There's a young man in front of us who can't keep his eyes off the woman. He's practically drooling over her Pilates-shaped legs and toned, exposed abs. I want to offer the young woman my jacket, but she reminds me of how I once dressed in Daisy Dukes and halter tops, cold weather be damned. We're all going to the same café, and the man eagerly steps aside to open the door for Pilates woman. She bats her eyelashes and thanks him. I smile at their cute exchange, not expecting the door that was opened less than a second ago to slam in my face.

"Oh, my bad, I didn't see you there," the man says as I open the door for myself.

There it is in full effect, the cloak of invisibility for the aging. I wave off his apology. I don't care if anyone opens the door for me. I have two very capable hands. It's his excuse that I find most irritating. How could he not have seen me? Is the fact that my ass isn't as tight or exposed really a good enough excuse to have a door slammed in my face? I get it. I'm in my seventies, not my twenties. I have the urge to slap the young man on the back of his head and scream, I am not invisible! I glare at the man flirting pathetically with the woman at the counter. I can't help but wonder, who did I not see at their age? That's the other part of the curse. I was once a part of the visible world who didn't see the elders around me.

By the time I spot Elena, my blood is boiling. I shouldn't be as angry as I am. I should be used to being treated like this, but I'm not. Breathe Juliet. You don't want to scare off your date before you even sit down. Elena's sitting in a dark corner with a book in her hand and her glasses perched on the tip of her nose. It's not my favorite spot in the café, but she looks so cute tucked away in the corner that I decide to let it go. She stands when she sees me.

"I hope you haven't been waiting long. I forgot to set my alarm," I say as I hang my coat on the back of my seat.

"No, not at all."

I glance over at the young man who is still trying his best to flirt with the young woman who looks like a Pilates instructor.

"Is everything okay?" Elena asks.

"It's just one of those days that remind you how the world sees you."

"And how does the world see you?"

"As someone who doesn't deserve to be seen apparently. But it's okay. I'm not gonna let others mess up my day. If they live long enough, they'll find out eventually. Then maybe they'll think about the ones they didn't see."

"Well if it means anything, I see you, and you look radiant." A slow smile spreads across Elena's face. She looks at me as if I still have that tight ass and tiny waist from my youth. Oh God, how long has it been since someone looked at me with eyes full of desire? Not since Roy, I suppose. A waft of warm coffee and cinnamon that always reminds me of the changing season circles around me. Although I prefer to be sitting by a window watching the leaves of the red maple drift to the ground, I'm enjoying the sight in front of me. We order hot beverages and pastries. Me a chai tea, Elena a black coffee.

"You know, when Kat first mentioned you to me, she couldn't stop talking about how great you are. She went on and on about you all going to the club. Honestly, I didn't believe her at first. But the more she told me, the more your story captivated me. I had to meet you. So I hope you don't mind that my niece and I set this all up."

My cheeks and chest become warm. Because of my painting career, I've met many people. I've always been easy to flatter, partly because I didn't grow up in a household where I received a gold star for everything, or even an acknowledgment for that matter. It's silly that hearing Elena say she's captivated by my story makes something stir in me. Something reminds me of the young girl sneaking off to the kissing dock.

"Kat's a sweet girl. I wish I were as spunky at her age."

"Me too. I'm sure I would've had more fun and wasted less time."

A waitress comes over with two cinnamon rolls. Elena scoops some of the icing off hers and licks the tip of her finger. Her lips are tinted red, and she has tiny tattoos across her hand. Who is this woman?

"So, have you been living here long?" I ask.

"No. What gave me away?" Elena has a great smile that makes me feel welcomed and, at the same time, makes my stomach do a little flip.

"Your coat is the thickest I've ever seen."

"I knew it. I just don't understand this weather. One month I had the air conditioning on high, and now there are flurries. It's not like this in Florida."

I smile. "I get it. I'm from Georgia, but I've been living up here longer than I lived down there. I guess I'm used to the seasons. I do always miss Georgia once the snow starts piling up on the streets. The snow's only nice during Christmas."

"Oh no, I don't think I'm gonna be able to handle winter. I might need to book my flight right now. I've only been up here for three months, and my bones are slowly warning me that if I don't get it together, and soon, they're going to make me pay." We laugh. She's naturally funny, and she can talk just as much as Kat.

"So, have you been dating long?" I ask.

"Just for a few months. A friend of mine thought I should give it a try. But it hasn't been so good."

"Really? Why not?"

"There just hasn't been a connection—a real one. It's also not so easy finding women to date at our age. It's not like this young generation who are so fluid with their expression. They're gonna make some interesting old people. Wish I could be around to see it. Maybe I'll come back as a tree or something to quietly observe the world."

"Me too actually. But I'd like to come back as a bird."

Elena takes a sip of her coffee. "A bird and a tree sound like a perfect combination."

"I guess we'll have to set a date for our next lifetime."

The twinkling lights and local artwork hanging on the wall fade away, while the chatter becomes muffled and distant, as if we're underwater. I forget about the earlier encounter with the young man. I even forget the fact that I'm out publicly on a date with a woman. Soft flutters in my belly, the easy laughter, and now the shameless flirting overcome any care about my surroundings, at least for now.

"You know, I must say it's refreshing to meet someone so open to going out on a date with someone of the same sex at our age. Kat was telling me that you were married to a man for a long time. What made you want to go on a date with a woman?"

Just as fast as I swooned, Elena brings me back down to earth with the question I knew was coming when I agreed to go on a date with a woman who just so happened to be an OG lesbian. It's a great question, one I would've asked if the roles were reversed. I don't want Elena to believe she's some sort of experiment, which was something I read about online, but I also don't know if I feel the need to explain myself. Why am I here with this woman? Why now? Why not fifty something years ago?

"I was married a long time to a man named Roy. He was the love of my life and my best friend. Before Roy, I had a younger love named Ruby. She was my best friend growing up. I've been going through this awakening journey, so to speak, for a while now. Part of that journey has been exploring my sexuality. And I realize that there's a lot to explore. I'm attracted to both men and women, and I suppose I always have been."

"That's incredible. I've been a lesbian for as long as I remember, and it was not always easy. I was in denial for a large portion of my life, growing up in a Catholic Cuban family."

"I get it. My mother always kept a Bible in hand." I remember all the nights I spent praying my feelings for Ruby away.

"My first marriage was to a man I met my first year in college. I was eighteen. We lasted two miserable years. After that, I decided I would rather be an outcast and live my life the way I wanted than be accepted but unhappy."

"I know that feeling. Not wanting to live with regret or what ifs."

"Exactly! And it sounds to me like that's what you're doing with your journey."

"Much later in life than you."

"There's no timeline for this type of stuff."

"You're right, there's not."

I take a slow sip of my tea and allow the spices to melt on my tongue. "So you're not married, you're beautiful and funny, and somehow you're still single. What's the catch?" Why are you asking her this, Juliet? Does it really matter why she's single? Am I simply fishing for something, anything that will make it more than easy to walk away and sabotage what could possibly be?

"No catch. I'm still single because I choose to be. I don't think I was good at relationships. I never wanted to commit."

"Then why did you want to go on a date with me?"

"Well, I never said I don't enjoy the company of a woman who is both stunning and incredibly talented. And if I hadn't come on a date, I would've missed out on all these wonderful questions."

I smile, feeling a little embarrassed for turning our first date into an interrogation. Have I not moved past this point in my life? Have I not learned how to surrender?

"Excuse my questions. But you understand how it is to be our age in this world. Sometimes you just—"

"Have to get straight to the point," she says, finishing my thought.

"Exactly. And are you sure you don't want one of these young, care-free women out here?"

"Oh no, I'm not looking to hold onto my youth. I'm not trying to fill a void with a woman who could be my niece. I want to spend time with a woman who has already lived a long life and appreciates what she has."

"Well, I'm not so sure that I've truly lived." I tear a piece of my cinnamon roll and pop it in my mouth.

"I find that hard to believe. But if it is true, a woman who can admit that she hasn't truly lived is usually on the brink of something incredible."

I'm intrigued by Elena. She stares at me as if I'm the most fascinating woman she has ever encountered, as if I genuinely enchant her. When I look into her eyes, I feel nerves rumbling throughout my entire body. I know how much of a catch I used to be. Am I still?

I turned many heads in my day. I used to strut around San Francisco in short shorts and cropped halter tops, or tight-fitting dresses that hugged all my curves. I was the shape of a coke bottle and so hard to get that I became the highest prize. Roy didn't know how to respond to all the stares and whistles in our early years of dating. It wasn't until I got married, had Toni, and moved to Ohio that I slowly became a quieter version of myself. I told myself it would've been selfish to dress the way I once did or be as daring as I used to be. All I wanted was to be better than my mother. I wanted the perfect family, even if it meant losing myself in the process. Who would've thought, at seventy-five, the part of myself I silenced would be screaming for release from the cage I put her in many years ago?

"Tell me more about your travels." I hope the change in subject will stop her from looking at me with those eyes. After taking a sip of her coffee, she sits back in her seat.

"My favorite two countries that I've been to are Brazil and India. I lived in each for years at a time. Brazil always reminded me of my home in Cuba, and India always grounded me in this world. Brazil is full of passion, and I'm not ashamed to say I had many love affairs on those beautiful beaches. I was a hippie, living out of a backpack, free love, wandering about in search of purpose, the Goddess, with long untamable hair that I still can barely get a comb through. My family hated it."

"I would love to have seen that."

"You would be greatly disappointed." Elena says with a laugh.

"I doubt that very much. What about now. Do you still travel?"

"Every once in a while. I usually split my time between here and Portugal."

"Why here? I would choose the Algarve over Ohio any day of the week."

"Yeah, it is beautiful there. I used to ask myself that question all the time. Why here? My parents moved us to the States from Cuba when I was a child, and I spent almost every year trying to escape. But the older I get, the more I like the simplicities of a small town. When my sister, Kat's mom, moved here years ago, I was struck by how peaceful yet colorful this town is. I also do my best woodwork and pottery here in this town."

I listen quietly to her stories. Every word has me leaning in for more details about her excursions through jungles and rainforests, her encounters with tribes all around the world, her daring adventures on mountaintops and beneath the sea. And her many rendezvous.

"Tell me about your travels."

I don't want to talk. I'm much more content listening to her speak. But this is a date, and I don't want to scare her off...yet.

"I've traveled all over, thanks to my art career. But I always felt guilty for being so far from home, away from my family. I went to lavish parties, underground, academic, you name it, with the big shots of the art world. But I could never truly enjoy myself. By the time people were staggering into a party, I was making up an excuse for why I had to leave. I did enjoy walking the streets of foreign cities. Most of the time, I was alone. Except one time when an old friend came to visit me in Ireland of all places."

"What were you doing in Ireland?"

"I was a guest speaker at an art conference."

"I'm sure you loved that."

"Oh it was horrible, but the country was beautiful."

"And your friend, were you happy to see them?"

"Surprised mostly. I hadn't seen this friend in years."

I remember it like it was yesterday. I was almost forty. Ruby said she looked me up at the college where I was teaching and saw I would be speaking in Ireland that week.

***

"It was an impulsive thing to do, I know, but I've missed you, Juliet. And I know I shouldn't be saying this because you're married. You made that very clear the last time we saw each other. I just...I don't know. I should leave." She turned around with her luggage in hand.

"You've come a long way to leave so soon. I was just about to order dinner. Stay." I walked back into my hotel room and left the door open. Before coming on the trip, I had yet another huge fight with Roy about traveling so much. We were fighting a lot those days. Divorce was mentioned on more than one occasion. So I must admit I was excited Ruby and not Roy surprised me on that trip.

She walked in slowly and set her bag on the floor by the door. Neither of us spoke. I made tea and lit a fire in the fireplace. The room was warm and cozy, but there was an obvious distance between us. I sat on the sofa across from her and watched her fidget with her coat.

"You know, the first time you showed up unexpectedly you had a black eye and a husband."

"Yeah well, I have neither of those now."

"I know. I remember. You're a long way from home, Ruby. You said you missed me, but you could've just called."

"Well, I called the last time and look how that turned out."

"I was engaged, and at least I told you."

"I know. Our timing is never right."

"Now that's the truth."

We stared at one another as I sipped my cup of tea.

"So why are you here now? You think the timing is right?" I asked.

"Maybe it's because we'll be forty soon and I'm going through a midlife crisis. I can't stop thinking about what could've been between us if I never would've left with George. Would we be growing old together? Would I be making you tea while you paint?"

"You came all the way to Ireland because of a fantasy you created in your head?"

"No, I came here for you, Juliet!"

Ruby stood up and walked closer to me. She knelt on her knees in front of me and grabbed my hands.

"I know that you're married. And I know that you have a child, and you take your roles as a mother and wife very seriously. I don't want to come between you and your family, but I also don't want to continue to live with what ifs. You can tell me to go, and you'll never have to see me again. But if you want me to stay..." She looked at me with those same big, round, blue eyes that always tugged at my heart. Did I want her to stay? My answer should've been no. My answer should've been hell no. I should've walked her to the door, thanked her for coming, and called Roy to check on him and Toni. I should've done a lot of things in that moment.

I knelt on the floor in front of her. I cupped her face in my hands and pulled her lips to mine. They were just as soft as I remembered. Although our bodies were softer than they once were, I still remembered every inch of her skin. Our clothes were off in a matter of seconds. She wore that familiar floral perfume on her neck and wrist. I wanted to touch her, taste her. And I did. Many times.

Somehow, we finally made it to the bed. She traced my body with her fingers. We caught up on life and talked for hours. George had died, and she'd remarried to a wealthy man named Carl. She received a lot of money from their divorce, which was how she was free to travel. Our conversation reminded me of all those years ago in that small apartment in California. Except this time, when Ruby talked dreamily about our future and what it would look like, I didn't respond. How could I have a future with her when my present was waiting for me back home?

"You've been quiet for a while. What's on your mind?" she asked. The glow from the pink sunrise danced against Ruby's skin. She'd always been so beautiful.

"I want you to leave."

"What?"

"You said if I wanted you to leave then you would, and I would never see you again."

"But that was before."

"I know. But there can't be a future with us when I still have one with Roy."

She stared at me without saying a word. There were too many words between us that needed to be said, but she knew from my face I was serious. She put on her clothes and grabbed her coat and luggage. As I walked her to the door she turned around. "Are you sure about this, Juliet? If you were truly happy in your marriage, would you have done what you did with me last night?"

"Yes, I'm sure. And happiness in my marriage has nothing to do with my choices last night."

"Then why did you do it?"

"Because I love you, Ruby. I've always loved you and I always will. But that's not enough to blow up my entire life!"

"You mean I'm not enough."

"That's not what I said."

"It's okay. I get it. I've been married twice now. I know how it goes." She kissed me on the cheek. "Goodbye, Juliet."

When the door closed, I collapsed onto the floor and sat there in a pool of tears. I didn't know if I was crying because I cheated on Roy and could never tell him or that I was sure I would never see Ruby again.

***

I don't know why I felt the need to tell Elena this story. It doesn't necessarily paint me in the best of light, especially during a first date when the whole point is to paint yourself in the best light possible so there could be a second date. I should've saved this story for date number four. Roy appears at the table in front of us. He's sitting there staring into his cup of dark-roast coffee.

"I knew you were different when you came back from that trip. But I never thought that was the reason why."

"I didn't want to hurt you. And we were already in such a rough patch that would've been the end."

He looks up and stares at me. "Shouldn't it have been? If the roles were reversed and I was with some other woman while you were away, you would've called it quits. But you just came back like nothing ever happened."

"I'm sorry, Roy."

"Save it. You got what you wanted. You took it to the grave. Just so happened to be mine."

He disappears before I can respond. I turn my attention back on Elena who hasn't stopped looking at me since I sat down. It makes me feel as if I'm under a spotlight. Are my palms getting sweaty?

"You probably think I'm some sort of harlot or something."

"No, I don't think that at all. I think you're a woman who's lived a life. Even if it wasn't perfect. I've had my own nonperfect moments. Many."

"Probably not as bad as cheating on your husband and never telling him."

"Worse actually. Imagine your long-term partner catching you in bed with her sister, who was married."

"Well, there you have it folks, we're just two old harlots sittin' in a café," I reply.

"Don't be so hard on yourself. The many mistakes I've made were some of the greatest lessons. They taught me how to become a better, kinder, more loving person. If I had the choice to make those mistakes all over again, I would do it in a heartbeat."

I'm starting to like Elena more and more.

"Elena! Is that you?" Lili walks past the table with her blueberry scone in hand. She gives me a quick smile, then does a wide-eyed double take.

"Juls, I didn't even see you there! You know Elena?"

"We just met yesterday evening," I can tell Lili wants more information, and I'm sure she'll be calling me tonight.

"How do you two know each other?" I ask.

"Oh, we met at mass years ago. I believe Elena was visiting her sister."

"Yeah, she even tried setting me up with one of her friends once. It ended in disaster, and I made her swear not to set me up again." Elena's smile is playful.

"My friends are lovely women, thank you!"

"Sure, but they are extremely dull and would date anything that moves."

"Well, you're sitting with one of my closest friends, and it sure doesn't look like you think she's dull." Lili looks at me again, but I can't meet her eyes just yet. I haven't told her about dating again or being attracted to women. Lili could've been a detective in a past life. The cat is most definitely out of the bag.

Elena smiles and looks at me. "You got me there. Juliet is far from dull."

"Well I don't want to keep you two from your *date*. You two kids have fun." Lili's wink is a sure signal that we're going to talk all about the encounter later.

Elena and I leave the café an hour later with full bellies. I'm more than prepared to call it a day and return home to take a nap, but she has other plans.

"Would you like to go dancing? There's this little jazz club that has fantastic music."

"But it's noon."

"This place opens early and stays open late. We'll practically have the dance floor to ourselves."

Leaves blow around my ankles as if they're speaking to me. Go, go, they whisper. I could make up an excuse as I've done on many occasions. I'm sure I can easily pull out one of my old lines. I have to wake up early in the morning. I need to check in on my daughter. I'm so exhausted that I can barely keep my eyes open.

Making excuses goes against my plan. I'm seventy-five, not twenty-five. If I don't want to do something, I don't have to lie to get out of it. I want to go. I love dancing, and I enjoyed my conversation with Elena. It doesn't hurt that she's easy on the eyes, and I can get lost in her stories for hours. I turn off my racing mind for a second to listen to what the swirling leaves are saying. Adventure. No regrets. Taking risks.

"I would love to go dancing."

She lifts her arm for me to take, and we walk to the jazz club in silence, listening to the high-pitched singing of the birds, the crunching of leaves under our feet, and the tiny paws of squirrels jumping from one tree trunk to the next. Elena has a subtle scent of cannabis smoke in her coat that's only noticeable when the breeze blows in our direction. We walk slowly, content with each other's company and in no hurry to get to our destination.

Chapter Twelve

ROY AND I DATED for a few years. He became my best friend, the person I turned to whenever I needed anything. He proposed marriage on more than one occasion. Of course I turned him down each time. Why ruin a good thing? We often went out on the town with Tommy and his beau of the week. I sometimes visited Roy at his job. He brought me dinner every Tuesday and Friday night. We never had much money, but somehow we always found a way to have a good time. Life was perfect until December 1969.

Roy was drafted to Vietnam. For the first time, I faced the reality that I might never see him again. I didn't sleep yet dreaded each new day. Each night I lay awake next to Roy, trying to soak in as much of him as I possibly could. My prayers fell on empty ears, because before I knew it, I was hugging him in a train station.

"I don't want you to go," I said, with tears in my eyes.

"Trust me, I don't wanna go, Peach."

"Are you scared?"

"A little. But the thought of you will keep me going. I'm coming back and making you my wife. We're gonna live in a nice house with kids. We're going to be a family. That's enough to keep me alive."

"You have to ask me again."

"Ask you what?"

"To marry you."

He smiles. "Juliet Livingston, will you marry me?"

The question sang from his lips.

"I will. I'll marry you, Roy."

He pulled out a string from his pocket and tied it around my ring finger, then swooped me up in his arms and kissed me so deeply I forgot we were in a train station.

The train whistle blew.

"You can wear this until I come back to give you the real thing."

"I'll wear it every day, and I'll be here when you get back."

He gave me one last kiss and walked off to board the train.

Months dragged by after Roy left. I tried to keep myself busy with odd jobs here and there. I didn't go out to parties. I didn't go out at all except to work. My days blended into one another, until a phone call one Saturday afternoon.

"Hello, Juliet speaking."

"Juliet."

Ruby. I hadn't heard from her since she left with George. I wanted to hang up the phone. I also wanted to hear what she had to say.

"Ruby?"

"I've been wanting to call you for so long."

"Can I help you with something?" I didn't intend for my tone to be harsh, but I couldn't help it. The hurt was still there, even after all those years.

"It's good to hear your voice."

"Why are you calling Ruby? Where's your husband?"

"Dead, actually."

I paused not expecting that answer. "I'm sorry to hear that."

"Don't be. He was an ass."

"Have you been doing, okay?"

"Yeah. I just miss you, and I'm sorry for how I acted. I'm sorry I didn't tell you I was married, and I'm sorry I left with him," she blurted out.

"We were supposed to grow old together," I whispered, as I twirled the phone cord around my finger.

"I know. I completely messed up everything. I was afraid to leave him. I think I was also afraid to be happy."

"Are you happy now that he's gone?"

"I would be happier if I were with you, like we planned."

The phone slipped out of my hand.

"Hello, Juliet."

"I'm here."

"So what do you say? If I were out in California, could we possibly start our life? The one we dreamed about."

"Ruby, I'm engaged."

She's silent for a while. "You're engaged?"

"Yes. His name is Roy, and I love him very much."

"Roy." There was a slight stutter to her voice. She was probably just as shocked as I was when her husband arrived at my door.

"Yes, Roy."

"Looks like our timing is off again. You think it'll ever be right?"

"I don't know, Ruby. I really don't. But it was good hearing from you."

"It was good hearing your voice, Juliet. Maybe we can keep in touch."

"That would be nice."

By the time I hung up the phone, my hands were shaking. All my feelings for Ruby resurfaced. I'd neatly tucked them away so I could function normally. There were so many things I wanted to ask her. What had she been up to for all those years? What were her plans now that her husband was dead? I was having a hard enough time as it was with Roy being gone. How could I deal with all my confusing emotions for Ruby? I called the number she'd given me.

"Hello?"

"Hello Ruby, it's Juliet."

"Juliet! I didn't think you would call so soon."

"When do you think you can come to the city?"

"I'm already here. I was hoping you would want to see me. I've been staying at a hotel for two days, trying to get up the nerve to call."

"Okay. Can you give me the address? I'll meet you there."

I stood outside Ruby's hotel for what felt like hours. My heart was being pulled between a room somewhere inside the hotel and a far-off land where I hoped Roy was still alive. I waited for a sign, one to tell me to go or one to tell me to stay. The longer I waited, the more I realized there wasn't going to be a sign. I needed to choose.

"Juliet."

Ruby stood at the hotel's entrance. Her face was sharper than when I last saw her, more defined. She'd cut her mid-back-length hair to a crop just past her ears. She looked like someone who belonged in the city, or on a magazine cover.

"Ruby."

We faced each other for the first time in years. I wondered how I looked through her eyes. Had I matured any?

"I'm glad you called back. I didn't think I would hear from you."

"I didn't think I would call so soon either."

"Why did you?"

I stuffed my shaking hands inside my jean jacket. "I don't know. I thought I had gotten over all my feelings for you and moved on with my life."

"Sounds like there's a but there."

"But anytime I hear your voice I think of our life together. I think about the dock on the lake back home. I think about us dancing at bars here or falling asleep to you snoring."

"I do not snore!"

"Sure you don't. You're hard to stay away from."

"What about your fiancé? What will he think?"

I looked past Ruby at the trolley going by. It's funny how quickly we can compartmentalize the thoughts and memories we want to forget. We store them away as if they never happened and continue with life.

"My fiancé is in Vietnam. I have no idea what he thinks. I wish I did."

"What if he comes back? Are you still going to marry him even if we get back together?"

I looked down at the string Roy had tied around my ring finger. That day in the train station felt so far away yet stuck with me like a recurring dream.

"I don't know if he's ever coming back." My voice was barely a whisper.

Ruby took my hand. "Come, it's starting to rain. We can have lunch and catch up."

I stared at my hand intertwined with Ruby's. Was that my final decision, to choose Ruby over Roy? I didn't have time to analyze all the questions that arose within me. My feet carried me inside the hotel, up the elevator, and into Ruby's room.

Two months went by. Summer was almost over, and the leaves were hinting change. I had settled into my new routine of work, sleep, and Ruby. When I was alone, I tried to distract myself, to forget.

"You've been going out quite a bit lately. Care to share where?" Tommy tossed a grape in his mouth while I applied eyeliner and mascara in the kitchen.

"Nope, not really."

"Oh come on, Juliet. You went from being a hermit to going out every night all dolled up. Who are you going to see when you leave here?"

"Tommy, I love you, but this is none of your business."

"For as long as we've known each other, we've never kept secrets about our love affairs. Why are you starting now? It's not like you're sneaking off with the one who shall not be named." He laughed.

My silence gave him the answer he was seeking, and his face quickly changed from playful to appalled.

"Wait, no. Not Ruby. You can't be talking about Ruby?"

"It's complicated, okay?"

"Might I remind you how miserable you were when she left you for her awful husband? What happened, he left her and now she's bored?"

"Actually, he's dead."

"Okay well that's very tragic and dark. But it still doesn't excuse the fact that she hurt you. And what about Roy? Have you forgotten about your fiancé already?"

"Of course I haven't forgotten about him!" I snapped. I tossed my makeup down on the table, no longer in the mood. "I don't even know if Roy is alive or dead! I have no way of knowing. All I can do is try to get through every day hoping he's okay and will find his way back to me. But that's not guaranteed, is it?"

"And you think *she's* guaranteed?"

"I think *she's* here. That's as far as I can think right now."

Tommy cupped my face in his hand. I didn't realize tears were rolling down my cheeks until he wiped them away and I saw the black mascara on his palms.

"Roy's coming back. You must believe that, Juliet. Wherever he is right now, he *needs* you to believe that."

I didn't want to keep listening to Tommy's lecture, mainly because I knew he was right. I didn't believe Roy was dead. If he were, I had a gut feeling I'd know somehow. But I had no idea when the war would be over. It could have been years before I saw him again, if I saw him again. I wiped my face and grabbed my purse.

"I gotta go. Don't wait up."

I met up with Ruby at a park. She wanted to have a picnic. The whole setup was really nice and romantic, but all I could do was stare at the anti-war protestors and think of Roy experiencing horrible things. Meanwhile, the girl he loved was on a date with someone else.

"Is everything all right, Juliet?"

"Sorry. I'm just a little out of it today. This is nice, but do you think we can go back to your place? Those protestors are a little distracting."

Ruby nodded. "Say no more. We can have an indoor picnic."

We packed up our belongings and headed to Ruby's hotel. But even the change of scenery couldn't erase the guilt growing inside me.

***

On a Tuesday morning, months after Ruby first came back to town, I sat curled up on the sofa reading a book. Tommy was cooking breakfast. We didn't talk about Ruby. He wouldn't even acknowledge she existed. I heard three knocks on the door.

"Who is it?" Tommy yelled out.

"Why don't you just go and see?"

"I'm the one cooking here. You can go, Miss Bookworm."

I plodded toward the door.

"Who is it?" I yelled out.

"You're fiancé!"

I hurried to open the door, not trusting my own ears. I had been dreaming about this moment every night since he left. I'd started to believe I would never see him again.

"Roy!"

I jumped into his arms and pressed my lips against his. Time stopped. If it weren't for Tommy, we would've been in that hall the whole day.

Tommy cleared his throat. "You two should get inside before the neighbors think we're running a brothel."

"Man, I've missed that sense of humor of yours. Come here, man." Roy pulled Tommy in for a hug.

"I'm just glad you're home," Tommy said.

I pulled Roy's bag inside. "Wait, how are you home?"

"Well, I'm officially deaf in one ear, and the other isn't in the best condition." He shrugged. "It could be worse."

"How, what happened?"

Roy sat on the couch and pulled me onto his lap. "You don't need to worry about all those details. All that matters is that I'm alive and I'm here. Everything else isn't important."

I met Tommy's eyes before he went back to cooking. "You're right. Everything else isn't important."

"Oh and I got this for you." Roy pulled out a gold engagement ring and slid it onto my finger. "Now you're official."

"I was official before." I looked at the gold ring wrapped around my finger.

"Yeah, but now everybody else will know you're official. What are you in there cooking, man, cause I'm starving."

Roy hopped up off the couch and walked into the kitchen. I was still looking down at my ring, when a sinking feeling crept into my gut.

The following morning, before I headed into work, I stopped by Ruby's hotel. When she opened the door, her face lit up like the sun. I didn't share her enthusiasm, and her smile faded.

"Is everything okay?"

"Yeah. Well, no."

"What's wrong?" She sat on the edge of her bed as I paced the room.

"He's back."

I could see the wheels turning in her head. "I see. And you're going to stay with him." It was more of a statement than a question, but I answered anyway.

"Yes."

"I just thought we were serious this time."

"We were, but that was before Roy came back. That was before I even knew if he was still alive."

"So what, was I just some placeholder?"

"No, of course not. But I am going to marry him, Ruby. Just like you chose your husband last time, I'm choosing my future husband."

"Oh I get it. So this is payback?"

"Not at all. I do love you, Ruby. It's just bad timing."

"When will there ever be a good time for us, Juliet?"

"I don't know."

I walked over to the bed and gave her a kiss on the cheek, then walked out of the room. Three weeks later, Roy and I were standing in the courthouse saying I do and preparing to move to his hometown in Ohio to start our lives together.

Chapter Thirteen

ELENA IS SUCH A beautiful name. Rolls off the tongue like a song. Since our date two days ago, I can't stop imagining how our next will be. Destiny doesn't want me to put all my eggs in one basket, so she already has two more dates confirmed for this week. How can they compete with Elena? How can I swoon so easily? Maybe I'm turning into the ladies at spades night. Am I too eager and willing to fall for anything that moves or anyone who compliments me and has a cute smile?

She's an incredible dancer. We moved our bodies as one until our feet ached. I've been floating since the moment we stepped onto the empty dance floor in the small, dingy jazz club. I've also been thinking a lot about Roy, about our first kiss and our last. About our love. Is it possible to have room in your heart for more than one person? I've asked that question many times, especially regarding Roy and Ruby. Am I truly ready for my heart to be cracked open and split into more pieces to share?

My confidence is high for my second date, and my nerves are nowhere in sight. I feel sleek and seductive, and only an all-black outfit can match a mood like this. I find a pair of long, crystal earrings an artist friend from Senegal made for me on my first trip there. I always thought the earrings were too flashy and that I would never have anything to wear them with. But I was drawn to how they glimmered in the sunlight, creating rainbows on the walls around me and against my skin. I apply a dark red to my full lips and grin at the sexy woman in the mirror. I do a small spin in my long, flowy tunic and bell-bottoms. Why didn't I go on a date sooner? Even if I never talk to any of my dates again, it's nice to get dressed up and be given compliments on more than just my paintings.

I wait outside Sapori for my internet date, who is late. Did he forget we were supposed to meet? The setting sun is providing little warmth, and I'm regretting my flowy outfit. I'm past the point of thinking pain is beauty. I prefer comfort and warmth.

"So where's this date of yours?" Roy appears on the bench across from mine, looking like he did when we were in our early twenties. I smile at his warm, medium-brown skin and clean-shaved face. He's barefoot and showing off his lean, muscular body. His eyes are bright and hopeful like they were before he was drafted. He was always the most beautiful man I ever laid eyes on.

"Late, apparently."

He nods and casually looks around. I haven't spoken to him since my date with Elena. He doesn't look upset, but I know that's just because I don't want him to look upset. An ache in my chest reminds me how much I miss him. This awakening journey I'm on still hasn't cured my very human emotions. I want to burst into tears. I want to wrap my arms around him and sit on his lap like I used to when we were young. He leans forward with his elbows on his thighs and stares at me.

"You know I want you to be happy, Peach. I can't do nothin' about the past. About what you did or what I did, or what we didn't do. None of that really matters anyway. I'm glad you didn't tell me. If you had, we wouldn't have spent a lifetime together. And I can't imagine not having spent a lifetime with you. So you keep goin' on these dates and redecoratin' the house and searching for Ruby. If all this is making you happy, I support you."

"You know I can never replace you, right?"

"I know."

"And you know you were the love of my life?"

"Yeah, and you were mine. We had some good times together, didn't we?"

"We did."

"I just wanna know one thing, Peach. How come you felt like you couldn't be yourself around me? The last time I saw you as colorful and flashy as you've been lately was when we first met. Why'd you hide this part from me for so long?"

I think about his question. Had I been hiding myself from him during our years together? I don't think it was intentional. I think I just got so lost in my roles of being a wife and mother, that somehow, this part of me slipped away.

An older white man, with a cane and a funny-looking tie, walks up to me.

"You must be Juliet?"

"What gave me away?"

"Well, for starters, that gorgeous face of yours." He smells like cheese and enjoys touching my arm more than I would like. I paste on a smile, happy he finally arrived.

My date, Joseph, hasn't stopped talking from the moment we sat down at our table. His bright-yellow-sheep tie clashes with his blue plaid shirt, and his glasses slide down his nose every time he opens his mouth. A straight, white hairpiece sits on the top of his head like a dead animal.

"I own a farm not too far from town and one of the goats got out. That's why I was a little late. Have you ever worked with goats? Of course not. A fine woman like yourself is probably used to places like this fine, Italian restaurant."

"Actually, I worked with goats and other farm animals when I was younger, down South. It's been a long time," I manage to say into his continuous chatter.

"You should come by my farm sometime. My sons wouldn't believe how pretty you are."

"Are they the ones that gave you that tie?"

"Oh this old thing, I bought this back in the eighties. My third wife hated it, but I got it anyway."

My body has gone from cool to burning hot. The date just started, and all I want to do is run out the door. Would it be appropriate to excuse myself to the restroom and sneak out the back somewhere? Or am I at the age where I no longer must care about hurting his feelings? I wish I was never taught ladies are always supposed to be polite. There's an internal war happening between my brain and body, and neither has the upper hand. As dinner continues, my body seems to be winning the battle.

"I have twenty chickens, two dogs, six cows, a donkey, nine goats, and a pig that likes to bite ankles.

"I usually go to Spring Oaks retirement community for my dates. There are some pretty desperate women there, I tell you. They're nothing like you. You're a mystery. You've barely talked this entire date. I can say that those women know what they want. By the end of a date, I'm able to give it to them, if you know what I mean. I guess all those years working on a farm pay off. It really keeps up your stamina.

"So, Juliet, do you know what you want?"

I keep waiting for the hair piece on his head to jump onto the table. His eyes are beady, like a predator sizing up their prey. He licks his lips and waits patiently for my response. Every flick of his tongue makes my stomach churn. Did he just wink at me? I grab my purse and leave cash on the table to cover the meal I barely touched.

"I have to go."

"Wait. Why? The date's not over yet."

"Actually, it is." Walking out of this restaurant door sure makes me feel free.

***

I'm approaching my third date this afternoon. When Destiny told me to meet the man at a yoga studio, I was confused. I enjoy dancing, walking, swimming. Yoga is useful but not something I enjoy and certainly not something I expect to do on a first date.

The only person in the studio is a shirtless young man in his late twenties or early thirties. The dark-brown skin on his perfectly sculpted body is glistening from sweat, and his tight shorts leave very little to the imagination.

"Oh, excuse me, I think I have the wrong address." I'm already backing out of the room.

"Wait. You're Juliet, right?"

I stop in my tracks and look at him. "Yes, I am."

"I'm Chris, you're date."

"No, that's not possible. I saw a picture of my date, and he could be your grandfather."

"Well if I'm being honest, that *was* my grandfather's picture."

I keep my hand on the knob of the door in case I need to leave quickly. I've seen documentaries about what can go wrong with online dating, and I don't want to take any chances.

"Young man, I'm not sure what you're trying to pull, but I'm going to leave now."

"Please don't. I saw your picture on the dating site, and I thought you were beautiful. I knew you would never go out with me if you knew my real age."

"That's because you could be my grandchild."

"But I'm not. I'm an adult man who's attracted to a woman older than him. All I'm asking for is one date."

He seems sincere. And wouldn't it be ageist if I walked away from the date without giving him a chance? If the roles were reversed, the answer would be a clear yes. In this case, is it possible I could just chalk it up to personal preference? I decide to stay, hoping curiosity won't kill the cat.

Chris guides us through a gentle yoga session accompanied by his playlist. Of course he's a DJ on the side. The stretches and breathing are relaxing, the lit candles create a soft ambiance, and the room smells like fresh lavender. But I refuse to let my guard down around someone who lied about who they are.

"I'm happy you stayed. I've been looking forward to this date all week." He brings me a bottle of water after the session, and we sit on our mats.

"Is that right?"

"Yeah, I mean, you're the finest woman I've been out with in a good minute."

"You don't say. If you don't mind me asking, how old are you?"

"Thirty." He has an overconfident smile. I'm sure he intended for the gaze moving up and down my body to come across as sexy and flirty, but the only thing I'm getting is creepy.

"Do you date often?" I ask.

"Yeah, I get around. But none of those women are my type."

"And what's your type?"

"I like my women mature."

"And by mature you mean?"

"Older."

"So, this isn't your first date with an older woman?"

He leans back and takes a sip of his water. "No, of course not."

"And this isn't your first time using your grandfather's picture, is it?"

He flashes me another smile. "Guilty."

I look around the yoga studio. "This is a very nice studio. It's yours, right?"

"Yep. Pretty fancy right? It's one of the best locations in town."

"And you said you're a DJ?"

"Yeah, up and coming."

"Are your parents well off?"

"No, not really. Pretty average I guess."

"The women you usually date, are they pretty well off, financially speaking?"

He leans back on his hands and looks at himself in the mirror.

"That is usually my type. I need someone to match my vibration, and that does include finances. I prefer to live in abundance."

I get up from my yoga mat and grab my bag.

"Wait, where are you going?"

"Home."

"I thought we were having a good time. I thought you were giving me a chance." His voice is on the verge of whining, and his face reminds me of a stray puppy.

"I did give you a chance. I'm not sure what type of *Harold and Maude* fantasy you have, but I'm not gonna be a part of it."

"So you're going to leave like all the others, just because I'm a little younger than you."

I chuckle. "Sweetheart, you're not a *little* younger than me. I'm not leaving because of your age. I'm leaving because you're a liar who paints himself as a victim. And I'm no one's suga mama." Once again, I walk out the door without looking back.

I need to see Elena to recover from my two failed dates.

***

"Wait, so he pretended to be his grandfather to go on a date with you?" Elena asks, as we walk along a park trail on a cloudy afternoon.

"Yeah, he did. And it wasn't his first time either. It was basically his only job that brought in actual money. The online dating world is a strange place."

"It definitely can be." She extends her hand for me to take, and I do without giving it a second thought.

Chapter Fourteen

LIFE FEELS DAMN GOOD, exploring the excitement of possibilities.

"I can't believe you've been going on dates for a month now. Has anyone caught your eye?" Destiny is sipping tea at my kitchen table. I feel like a butterfly fluttering from flower to flower in an old, sage-green kimono. I sit down and wave my hand like I'm shooing away the notion.

"Elena and I have been talking a bit, almost every day. We've gone on a few more outings. But nothing major yet, no need to complicate it."

"Okay, Grandma. I see you, keeping things all casual."

"I surely am. I'm hip. You're just getting to see me in a different light."

"Yeah, you're right. Really though, I'm so proud of you. What you're doing is brave. You know how many people are afraid to live their lives the way they want to. You're an inspiration, and you look happier than you've looked in years...since Grandad."

I reach over to squeeze Destiny's hand. "I feel happier."

"I'm sure you're probably not thinking about this right now, since you're all booed up and everything, but I haven't found Ruby yet. I'm gonna keep looking. I've got some friends helping, who are techier than me. It might take some time. Honestly, at the rate it's going, we might not find anything."

At the mention of Ruby's name, I lean back in my chair and gaze out at the snow flurries beginning to fall. The trees are bare, and I must look at the calendar on my refrigerator to remind myself that it's already November. Time is moving quickly. Watching the small flakes makes me think of Elena. and our conversation about how she used to hate winter unless she had a woman to share it with. A memory of Ruby halts the chuckle trying to rise from my chest. When we were children, she always wished she could see the snow.

Ruby has been the center of my journey. I wanted to find her. I hope she's had a long and fulfilled life. I hope she lived the life of her dreams. I wonder if, just maybe, somewhere deep down, I've been a part of those dreams. How selfish can I be to want her to long for me? I was the one who didn't follow through. On multiple occasions. How selfish! Fear creeps up my spine, making me sit upright. I don't want to alter Ruby's life more than I already have, no matter how much time has passed. Haven't I done enough?

"You know what, that's okay, sweetie, you don't have to keep looking for her."

"Why not? It's not impossible to track her down. It just may take some time. Some older people are on social media, and some aren't. But my friends are good at finding people."

My eyes wander back over to the window.

"Are you afraid of the possibility of not finding her?" Destiny asks.

"No, I'm afraid you *will* find her. I'm not the same person I was when I last saw her. What makes me think she will be? What makes me think she wants to be found? Sometimes it's best just to leave things in the past."

"Grandma, it's okay. We can find h—"

"I said no!"

Destiny flinches at my sharp voice. I've never raised my voice at her. There are too many emotions and too many thoughts running through my mind. I've worked so hard, chipping away at my cement mask, I no longer know how to pretend to be okay. I've unlocked my emotions to feel the fullness of life, and now I don't know if I can control them.

"Maybe you should go. I just need to get some rest. I'm not feeling too well."

Destiny's face is pale. "Okay Grandma. I love you. Get some rest."

"I love you too, Destiny. I'll call you."

Destiny closes the door behind her. I listen for the sound of her car leaving before I curl up on the couch in front of the fireplace. I watch the flames and listen to the wood pop and crackle. The fire helps warm the cold numbness that has taken over my body, at least temporarily.

I allow myself a day to stay in a funk. If I go past a day, it will be harder to leave this dark space. I've been sleeping and reading my favorite Gwendolyn Brooks poems in my comfiest, white-cotton pajamas. My blank canvases disgust me, so I've tended the fire and spread homemade blueberry jam on some toast.

"Why so blue? Did somebody die?" Roy's sitting with his feet up on the couch, looking as he did when we were in our fifties. That was right around the time I sunk into a dark hole after my father died.

"No, no one died."

I don't look at him. I don't want to talk. I want to remain in my funk for however long I want to and come out the next day bright and new as if nothing had happened.

"It's about her, isn't it?"

I don't respond. My nose remains pointed down at my book, as I reread the same sentence over and over again.

"I know we haven't talked about her much. But you're not on this journey because of her. You're on it for you. You can't just stop living cause you ain't found her."

"And what do you know? If I wanna sulk, I'll sulk."

"But who's gonna get you out of the funk this time? I was here when you lost your dad, but when I was gone, it took you years. Don't do the same thing when you don't even know if it's worth it."

"Roy can you just leave!" I slam my book closed and look up to find an empty couch. I don't want a lesson on life. I want to experience all my emotions. Doubt. Sadness. Fear. All of it. Just because I'm on this journey doesn't mean I'm above all that comes with it.

It's dark outside, reason enough to go to bed. It's probably the moon. I always blame the moon for any emotions I have that are out of the ordinary. I don't know what it is about nighttime, warm blankets, and the secrecy darkness holds. Surprisingly, the throbbing sensation returns between my thighs.

"Really? Tonight?" I whisper.

Today is a day for sulking, not to think about how nice it would be if someone were lying next to me underneath the covers. Where is this even coming from? I know grief can make people hornier than usual. After my father passed, Roy and I went at it like rabbits for months. Sex was a great distraction from my inner world. Maybe I'm grieving the possibility of not finding Ruby. I didn't prepare myself for not finding her. It's like watching her walk out of that bed-and-breakfast in Ireland all over again.

The thought of Roy lying next to me comforted me for years, but there were never any tingles, just a numb, empty void. I crave a warm body, someone who can appreciate the wrinkles underneath my clothes just as much as I'm learning to. I want to be held and touched and kissed. I want to forget, just for a second or two.

Elena picks up on the first ring. "Hello, Juliet, are you okay?"

"I'm fine. I just can't sleep. Sorry I missed your call earlier. I needed some time away from everyone." I sit up in my bed and look out at the waxing moon.

"I understand. I'm just glad I get to hear your voice. Besides, I'm a night owl. I'm the perfect person to stay up late with."

I feel like a teenager sneaking off to talk to my crush, without the massive shame and guilt. I like Elena, I really do. But I'm not ready to tell anyone about her besides Destiny and Lili. I want to keep her all to myself without the input of outside forces. By forces I mean my lovingly nosy daughter.

"Did you see the flurries?" I ask.

"Did I? I walked outside this morning to check the mail, and my slippers were soaked from the snow!"

"I wish I could've been there to see it."

"Oh really? Why, so you could've laughed in person?"

"Of course, but also so I could've made you some tea and covered you in a blanket to keep you warm."

"Is that right?"

"That's right."

"Well, I'm a little cold right now."

"Too bad you're not here. I'm a master at starting a warm fire." My imagination is wandering.

"You know we've never been to each other's home."

"That's true."

"It's been a while since our first date."

"Yes, it has," I admit.

"And I've enjoyed our daily phone calls, immensely."

"Why does it sound like there's a but at the end of that sentence?"

"Because there is. We haven't been on a date in over a week. I'm sure you've been busy with some of your other dates, but I want to see you again, Juliet."

I smile. "It's like you were reading my mind. Come to my house."

"When?"

"Tonight." There's no hesitation in my voice. I know what I want.

"Tonight, are you sure? Isn't it kinda late?"

"I believe the kids call it a booty call or is it Netflix and chill?"

Elena breaks out in a fit of laughter that lightens an already happy mood. Before I know it, she agrees to drive out into the snow to visit me.

"Should I bring an overnight bag?"

A sly smile spreads across my face. "I think you should."

We hang up and I immediately get to work, straightening up the house and my room. I didn't clean as much as usual today. Thankfully, my home is never messy. I put on sage, silk pajamas I bought a week ago for a rainy day—or a snowy night. The beautiful, sakura flowers hand-painted all over the fabric make me feel sexy and like I'm a part of nature in spring. I was always self-conscious about wearing such gaudy things around Roy. He was a humble man who worked as a janitor, then a sanitation worker until he retired. He couldn't afford to buy me the expensive gifts from my trips abroad. It wasn't as if I asked for them. The last thing I wanted to do was show off gifts worth a down payment on a house, or a couple of houses. I tucked them away in a trunk in my art room. I take them out occasionally, to reminisce about people and places I was fortunate to know. I was taught that a man's ego is as fragile as good china. Once it breaks, it's hard to put the pieces back together. I wish I hadn't tiptoed so much around his ego. He probably would've loved to see me in all my pretty clothes. He would've been more excited to take them off me, but I didn't give him the chance. All because I created a story in my head. Deep down, I was afraid if I didn't keep Roy happy, he would leave like my father left my mother.

I already have a cozy fire going when Elena rings the doorbell. I've been giving myself pep talks and doing my deep, belly breathing to remain calm. It's just Elena, for goodness' sake. I've been talking to the woman for the past month like we're old friends. There's no need to be nervous. But there hasn't been anyone in my house in this way since Roy. Snap out of it, Juliet, and open the door!

"Did someone request a sleepover, because I brought wine?" Elena stands on the other side of the door, bundled up, with flurries scattered through her grey hair.

"Music to my ears." I step aside so Elena can come in from the cold. I take her coat and overnight bag, as she makes herself more comfortable.

"Your home is beautiful, and it smells wonderful. Look at all the art, the colors. Are any of these paintings yours?"

"No, of course not. I always thought hanging up my own pieces was tacky."

"I've seen your paintings. They're far from tacky."

"Are all Cubans this good at flattery?"

She shrugs. "Perhaps. Romance does run through our blood."

"Well let me show you around, Ms. Romance."

I give her a brief tour of the house before we find our way to the couch. We settle into our usual comfortable silence as we gaze into the fire. The yearning I've felt to be close to Elena since our first date hasn't subsided and is being fed by the excitement of having someone over so late. I keep stealing glances at Elena to make sure she's really here.

"What made you want to become a painter?"

"I always enjoyed watching the world. When I was a little girl, I wanted to hold onto the image of different things I would see, things that made the world beautiful. I started painting when I was around eleven. My father bought me some brushes, paint, and a notebook and told me to fill it with everything I saw. He also gave me a book of all these different paintings and sculptures. I was hooked. My mother said everything I painted looked like a chicken. She was only angry my father was the one to introduce me to something I was good at."

"My parents never suggested I do anything remotely artistic. They went on and on about all the things they had to sacrifice to give me the life I deserved. The guilt of having immigrant parents I suppose."

"I understand. I know a thing or two about guilt."

"Isn't it funny how, even at our age, our childhood still has a lasting impact on us?"

"It is. There used to be days when I would wake up and wish I could forget my entire childhood. Then all the good memories would flood my mind, and I think it could've been worse."

"That's true. My father could've been a sloppy drunk. Instead, he was just a sloppy gambler."

We laugh at our childhood and agree we have only two choices. Either we can take the resentment to our graves or laugh and let it go.

"Is your mother still living?" I ask.

Elena shifts some in her seat. "No, she died when I was eleven. My father never remarried. He always said she was the love of his life. When the time came for him to die, he didn't want her to find out he remarried and kill him."

She smiles, but her eyes become distant as she stares at the fire. I gently lay my hand on top of hers...warm, soft but bony, and familiar as if, somewhere in another life, our hands had fitted into one another's many times.

"My mother passed away when I was seventeen. She was sick. I was supposed to go off to college around the same time she was diagnosed, but I stayed behind to take care of her. She wasn't the best mother for most of my childhood. I try to convince myself that I did the right thing. If I hadn't stayed, I wouldn't have the life I've lived. But there are times I wish I would've just left."

"You made the right choice. Sometimes parents that aren't the best end up with the sweetest of children, ones they don't deserve. If you had left and had to return for her funeral, it would've eaten away at you for the rest of your life."

I don't know how we got on the topic of our parents and families. I rarely talk about my mother to anyone, especially not to someone I've only known for a month. Something about Elena makes me keep baring my soul and laying out all my secrets for the light to see. Holding hands with Elena by the warm fire feels safe to open up, to be seen. I haven't felt safe in a long time.

"I like you, Elena, and it terrifies me to say that. The more I live, the more I understand how much of a gift time is. If I don't use this gift right now, God or whoever's out there will take it away." My voice trembles but I continue.

"I was in a dark place after Roy passed away. Life lost its purpose, its color. It wasn't until my birthday this year that I realized how much time I've wasted. I don't want to do that any longer. That's why I invited you here. That's why I'm telling you that every time you look at me, all I want you to do is press your lips against mine."

"Is that what you want me to do right now?" she asks with a soft smile.

"You're lookin' at me, aren't you?"

There is still a little wine in Elena's glass when she carefully sets it on the table in front of her and slides over until her leg touches mine. She leans over and brushes her lips on mine. The tingles have taken over my entire body. I want more. More of her. More parts of our bodies touching. I get up from the couch and walk toward my room. I stop and look over my shoulder with a playful smile dancing on my lips. "Are you coming?"

I light two candles as Elena undresses. She doesn't hurry to take off her clothes. Her eyes follow my every movement. She wants me to watch her. She extends her hand and pulls me close to dance to the sounds of the night outside the bedroom window. Hooting owls and gently tapping branches serenade us. She wears nothing but white underwear and a small pendant of the Virgin Mary. Her body is toned for a woman in her seventies. She must have been an athlete in her younger years, or maybe it's all that woodwork she does. The Hindu Goddess, Kali, covers her spine. The small peace sign on the inside of her wrist is faded. Slowly, Elena leans in to kiss the side of my neck. Suddenly, my pajama top buttons are popping off, one by one. My pants are now at my ankles. My initial response is to grab the blanket off the bed and cover my body, hyperaware of all my body's imperfections.

"Maybe I should blow out the candles." I pull away and head toward the nightstand, but she grabs my wrist and pulls me back to her.

"Don't you dare. I want to see you. I want you to see me. You're the most beautiful woman I've ever laid eyes on."

"You're just saying that."

Her warm palm on my cheek draws my focus to her serious voice. "No, I'm not. I mean it, Juliet. You're extraordinary."

The air from the fan in the corner of my room gently caresses my bare back. Goosebumps rise all over my body, and my arousal intensifies. I'm as exposed as on my birthday, when I saw myself in the mirror. I want Elena's hands to explore the entirety of my body instead of my own. She slips off her underwear and cups her hand around my right butt cheek. A playful giggle escapes my lips, as we make our way to the bed. She kisses every inch of my body. Her movements are like rhythmic waves, her tongue, her hands. A dance has taken over our bodies, and we're so in sync that I forget this is our first time together. I lift my chin to the sky, grab hold of the blanket beneath my hands, and silently pray, Please don't let the sun come up too soon.

Now I understand the other women at spades night. I, too, yearn for more toe-curling moments like this one. We lay in bed, wrapped in each other's arms underneath thick covers. We're watching the snow fall below the light of the moon. Elena is only my third lover. Just like riding a bike, my legs had a slight tremble in the beginning. The more I pedaled, the more I flew.

Chapter Fifteen

WHO SAYS WOMEN DON'T enjoy sex as much as men? I enjoy it very much, even if I was taught I shouldn't talk about how much I enjoy it. Not in public anyway, and certainly not with anyone besides my husband. I enjoyed sex with Ruby. I enjoyed it with Roy, and I'm enjoying sex with Elena. Making love at the sweet age of seventy-five isn't like how it used to be. It's better. I know exactly what I like now. I know where I like to be touched and how I like to be touched. And I'm not ashamed of how often I want to be touched. I didn't know anything about my body with Ruby, and I didn't know about hers. It was exciting to explore one another. Like many teenagers exploring sex for the first time, our lovemaking floated on the surface without exploring the deep, sensual, mind-expanding places one can go.

I didn't experience any of those expanding places with Roy until my mid-thirties. I was so concerned with making sure he was taken care of and that he was receiving pleasure, I didn't realize I was receiving the bare minimum. Like many women of my generation, I was taught a man's needs come first. I'm ashamed to admit this, but I became very good at faking.

I came across an article in one of those women's magazines. Women not having orgasms and being dissatisfied with their sex lives was a big topic for the eighties. I read that article with the intensity of someone stranded in a desert gulping down water for the first time. I was never taught about orgasms or the parts of my body and movements I could do to experience one. Toni was well into her school years and yet it took a magazine at my doctor's office to realize I wasn't experiencing all I could when I made love to my husband. My pleasure was just as important as his. After some time, with a little practice, I experienced those deep, sensual, mind-expanding places.

On the other hand, Elena felt like an explosion of pent-up energy. I didn't know if I still had it in me, but I'm happy to report I do.

***

I'm preparing for another online date with someone named Frank. The air is unforgivably cold, and I'd much rather be cuddled up on my couch, reading in front of the fire or talking to Elena. Winter makes me want to hibernate like a bear in their cave. But I promised Destiny I would keep my options open until I become serious with someone. And I must admit I always get a little excited about getting dolled up to go out with someone new. What should I wear? I dab a drop of perfume on my wrist and the side of my neck, waiting for an outfit to jump out from my closet and make my heart flutter. Very few pieces scream date material. The only outfit that truly resonates with my blossoming spirit is the yellow dress I wore for my birthday. I decide to wear it once more, paired with my long, patchwork wool coat.

I prefer being colorful and jazzy these days, even if others think it's too much. I don't identify with the boring old woman who only wears white and beige turtlenecks, even if I am perpetually cold. I no longer save dressing up for special occasions. Shouldn't every occasion be special? I make up my mind to wear the biggest pair of earrings in my secret trunk of treasures, and the most colorful blue-and-green pashmina scarf to wrap around my shoulders. I give myself a once over in the mirror.

"You're no boring pigeon, Juliet."

I sit at my vanity to trim my sideburns and shape up my hair. I apply my favorite dark lipstick, then dab a tiny bit on my cheeks as blush.

The bright scarf draped around my shoulders and the blue feather earrings dangling from my ears remind me of one of my favorite birds. I first saw the painted bunting when I moved to Ohio with Roy. I had to remind myself to breathe when it landed in front of me. A sign, I thought, without knowing what the sign meant. What I did know was that I had never seen a bird so beautiful, as if God had personally chosen the bird to be a canvas of color. As I stare at my reflection in the mirror, I finally feel as if God has chosen me as well.

Because this isn't my first blind date, my nerves are nowhere in sight. I'm a veteran after all. Destiny's been texting some pointers, since my other online dates were complete disasters. I get a real kick out of her texts. There must've been a time when I was bold enough to advise those who have been both where I was and where I was trying to go. I appreciate the advice nonetheless. I sit at a corner table between a window and bookshelf, in the same coffee shop where Elena and I had our first date. It dawns on me that I probably should've chosen a different spot. There's a possibility I might see her here, but I love their chai tea.

"Juliet?" My stomach flips at the deep voice behind me. A tall man with dark-brown skin, slender frame, and a white beard steps into view, his hands tucked in his coat pockets.

"Yes."

"I'm Frank."

"Yes, of course! Please sit, sit."

"This may sound strange, but I am so happy that you are who your online profile says you are." He has a lovely smile. Is this man a model? What on earth is he doing in Ohio?

"Not strange at all. I just recently experienced what kids call a catfish. He was definitely not who he said he was."

"You are even more beautiful in person."

"Thank you. So are you. I've been sitting here wondering how you're single."

"I could say the same about you."

"Yes, but I know the women in this town. If they saw you walking around, they would be on the hunt."

His laugh matches the merriment in his eyes. "Yes, there are some assertive women in this town. But right now, I'm here with you. And I want to get to know you better."

We talk about art and jazz and our favorite authors. He was a music teacher straight out of college and lived in Brooklyn until about five years ago. Our conversation is just as easy as my first date with Elena. It feels as if I'm talking to a long-lost friend. But every time I look at Frank, I can't help but think of Roy. They don't favor each other. They don't even act similarly to one another. I didn't have this same feeling with Elena. I never once compared her to Ruby. I suppose Roy and I went on a lot more dates than me and Ruby. The longer I sit at this table, the more I yearn for the dates I can no longer have with Roy.

Our conversation continues for a while. We don't realize the time that's passed until the waitress tells us the coffee shop is about to close.

"Would you like to join me for a walk?" he asks.

"Of course," I tighten the scarf around my neck.

We walk through the small town center, passing some of my favorite shops. I love to browse the art store and bookstore. We walk into the chocolate and wine shop and look around. My gaze falls on a bag of cacao from Guatemala, and I'm instantly taken back to the first time I came to this shop with Roy. The shop had just opened, and everyone was so excited to see what would be in stock. Toni was at a sleepover, so Roy and I had an impromptu date night. I dragged him to a movie and promised we would buy his favorite chocolate if he stayed awake throughout the film. Really, it was a win-win for both of us. I got to see what type of wines they were selling and Roy got to eat chocolate. As we were walking though the store, Roy picked up a bag of cacao nibs.

***

"C-A-C-A-O. I don't know how to say it. This looks like the real deal. Not that stuff in the grocery store."

"Aren't you glad I brought you here?" I say with a coy grin.

"Oh, don't try to use that smile on me. You brought me here so you can buy a new bottle of wine."

"I am not ashamed. Chocolate and wine are a perfect combination."

***

I had never heard of cacao prior, but every time I hear or see the name, I think of Roy.

"Do you want to buy some?" Frank reaches to grab the cacao in front of me. I forgot he was there.

"I'm not sure."

"The women in my yoga class rave about it. They drink it during their full moon gatherings. Lots of twenty-year-olds with moon tattoos and piercings."

The image prompts my giggle. "Sounds like a fun class."

"It can be, once I get over how bendy this younger generation is and how much my body just wants to stay home."

"I understand completely."

Frank buys a bottle of red wine, while I surprise myself and buy the bag of cacao. We walk around town a little bit longer before the cold becomes unbearable.

"Before I get frostbite, I think we should probably call it a day." Frank is visibly shivering.

"I think that's a good idea. The cold can be intense this time of the year."

"I really enjoyed our date. We should do it again."

"That would be nice."

Frank leans in and hugs me. We linger for a second in our embrace. I wait for that feeling to come, the one that says I must see this person again. I wait for my body or my mind to want to cook with this person, dance with them, have them in my bed. The feeling never comes. After we pull apart and I watch Frank's brisk steps to his car, I realize I may never follow up on that second date offer.

When I make it home and start a fire, I stand in front of the warm, amber glow and untie the bow around the bag of cacao. I inhale, as a single teardrop falls onto a piece of chocolate.

Chapter Sixteen

WHEN YOU'RE MARRIED for as long as I was, you learn that, over time, relationships develop their seasons. The beginning of my relationship with Roy felt new and fresh like spring. We were birthing something together and planting seeds without knowing or caring when the harvest would be. Our love was young and exhilarating, and we were going at it like rabbits. There were no responsibilities, no expectations, we simply enjoyed being around one another. I liked listening to his laugh. Roy used to say that he could watch me walk across, out, and back into a room all day. The little things gave us joy.

Our summer came with a new state, new house, new jobs, new friends, Toni, and a new life as parents. We basked in the life we made together. Those summer days were magical, hot, and oftentimes exhausting. We may not have been going at it like rabbits, but the flow we were learning to master still provided us with joy.

Summer went away as quickly as it came. Life started to slow down. We had responsibilities, obligations, someone outside of ourselves to keep alive, lights to keep on. We were forced to learn how to balance everything or risk everything falling apart. Our life was comfortable. Compared to many of my friends who stayed back home in rural Georgia, we had "made it" as a young Black couple living the American dream. All we were missing was the white picket fence. We had to plan when we had sex. Holidays and birthdays were usually the best time. I was starting to soar in my painting career. Roy was in and out of work. He lashed out, in the privacy of our room, from a wounded male ego unable to be the provider. I pelted him with complaints about the lack of support and freedom I needed for my career as an artist. In public, we were perfect. Behind closed doors, our leaves were quickly falling.

I didn't want him to touch me in our ice-cold winter. Our lovemaking became scarce. We were more like roommates than lovers, more acquaintances than husband and wife. I traveled more, taking Toni with me as often as I could. He took on longer shifts at his new job. From time to time, we remained still long enough to talk, to cry and laugh with one another. During those moments, we became as bare as the branches of the trees and let dry seeds fall and prepare our journey into a blossoming new spring.

I say all of this because I am now in an intimate relationship with a woman I care deeply about. Although newly beginning, we seem to have skipped spring. Our relationship is slow and sensual. She stimulates the depths of me I oftentimes keep hidden from others. Our relationship is rooted in friendship. There's no pressure, no expectations. We don't have to argue about children or when we're going to get married. We've already had long careers and no longer need to worry about financial stability. We've worked hard in our lives, and we're past uncertainties of life's younger years. Our energy is solely used for being with one another.

My relationship with Elena is feeding a part of me I didn't know was hungry, starving even. The other day, she made a stunning, five-course meal. She's an excellent cook and was once a top chef. With each course, Elena named an activity one of us had to do to the other. She called it an experimental dining experience. For the main course, I had to take off all her clothes and replace them with an outfit made of what was on the plate. For dessert she had to lick chocolate sauce off a part of my body. Exactly what part was up to me. The game was silly and a little kinky at times. We barely ate, but we did ravish each other until the early hours of the morning. I felt as wild as when I was nineteen, and I loved every second of it.

The other day, I walked into a lingerie store and bought a red satin nightgown with lace in the shape of flowers across the breast. Elena has invited me to spend the night for the first time, and I want to look elegant, but sexy.

Large windows wrap around her modern, Zen-like home in the middle of the woods. Being indoors while surrounded by nature feels like a luxurious camping trip where I can truly embrace the wild woman within. There's no need to worry if the neighbors might hear. We spend the evening dancing to our favorite classic songs and eating the delicious meal Elena made.

Elena lit a fire, and we're lounging on the comfiest sheepskin rug I've ever encountered. She pulls out a small wooden box, and I watch her fingers masterfully roll a joint as if she's been doing it for a long time. Knowing Elena, she probably has. I kiss her cheek, then walk to the bathroom to change into my nightgown. When I return, Elena is blowing rings toward the fire.

"I grow this myself, out back. I treat those little plants like they're my babies."

I steal the joint from her hand and take it to my lips. "Well I guess I'm in good hands then."

She stands up and rests her hands around my waist. I blow the smoke into her open mouth, and she presses her lips against mine. Now I must say, I haven't smoked marijuana since I was in my early thirties. I smoked it plenty in my younger years, but oh my how times have changed. It's much stronger than I remember, and it doesn't take long for my body to loosen. Any insecurities I had about the red nightgown fade. I'm at ease, safe, sometimes laughing uncontrollably, and oh so horny. This will be a night to remember if the grass doesn't make everything too fuzzy. I'm sure it's going to be fun.

***

Sometimes, when Elena isn't here, I do wonder if I'm ready to go through all the seasons with someone else again. Am I a coward if I don't open myself to allow for whatever to happen? Will I regret not diving deep into my new relationship to see how far it can go, or will I regret diving too deep and causing myself heartbreak? Can't I just have an everlasting summer with her?

I sit contently with both the joker cards in my hand. I'm now a regular at spades night, and I've become quite close with Shirley and Victoria.

"Thank you for these two books!" I high five Shirley when my partner and I win the third game in a row.

Lili sucks her teeth and opens another bottle of wine. "Okay, I'm starting to think you two are cheating. You know Shirley used to be into that bruja stuff back in the day."

"I was never into it. I was just dating someone who was. Everyone was into some type of stuff back in the eighties."

"Yeah, yeah. Speaking of stuff, I wanna hear more about what stuff Ms. Juliet is getting into these days. Or better yet who's, because someone in town saw you on a date with someone who's name rhymes with plank." Victoria prods.

"Who? Frank?"

"Yes, Frank."

Shirley's eyes pop out of her head. "Wait, you're dating Frank? Deep-brown skin, suave, good with his hands Frank?"

"How do you know he's good with his hands, Shirley? He never touched you," Lili challenges.

"I know these things. I always had a sixth sense of being able to just look at a man and tell if he's good with his hands. If his nails are dirty or longer than mine, that's a definite no. And if his hands are softer than mine, that's another no, because he's not gonna want to put some work in, and Mama needs hard workers!"

We all burst out laughing. It almost brings me to tears imagining Shirley on all of her dates, examining the guy's nails before they can even open their mouths.

"I'm not dating Frank. We went on one date, that's all."

"But Frank is a catch. When I first moved into Spring Oaks, all of the women knew him. He plays all sorts of instruments and draws a flock of women when he performs at Spring Oaks from time to time. He's always well-mannered, but no one ever caught his eye. We just figured he liked thirty or forty-year-olds," Shirley says.

"Frank is a nice man," I agree.

Shirley perches her cards in her palm and leans forward on the table.

"But there's someone else isn't there? Because I was just telling Victoria that there's something different about you and it must be a man."

My toes curl slightly, as I think of Elena and our times together. "There is someone."

Shirley snaps her fingers. "I knew it!"

"But it's not a man."

Victoria almost spits out her wine before the table goes silent. Lili continues to shuffle the cards, glancing at the other ladies. I don't know why I felt the need to tell them. Maybe I'm just feeling so damn good after all the time I've been spending with Elena that I no longer feel the need to hide. I'm not ashamed. I'm not sixteen years old sneaking kisses in the church basement.

"A woman?" Victoria takes another sip of wine.

"Yes, a woman. She's lovely. Her name is Elena."

"You know, I once dated a woman," Shirley muses.

Victoria whips her head around with wide eyes. "What? You?"

Shirley shrugs. "I lived in New York City in the eighties. Keep up Vicky. There's not much I haven't tried."

"Well, I may not be as liberal as you all, but I am happy for you, Juliet. Now if only *I* could find a man with good hands. You think Frank would go on a date with me?" Victoria sighs.

"I think he may smell the desperation a mile away and run," Lili teases, and Victoria tosses a piece of popcorn at her.

"You know you could sign up for online dating. That's how I met Frank. My granddaughter signed me up, and I've been going on dates since." I nonchalantly pop a piece of popcorn into my mouth.

"They have that for folks our age?" Victoria pulls out her phone and scrolls to the app store.

"Yeah, it's strictly for fifty and up. Most of the dates I went on weren't that great, but there's some nice men on there."

"You have to get Destiny to come by and set one up for each of us!" Shirley squeals.

"Nope, speak for yourself, hands lady. I am perfectly happy being alone. I don't have to share a bed with anyone or worry about what someone else is going to eat for dinner. I can come and go as I please," Lili says.

"But don't you miss late-night cuddles or gossiping to your husband who pretends not to like it but deep down can't wait for you to tell him all about the neighbors?" Victoria asks Lili.

"No. I don't miss any of that. I've come to enjoy my routine and my own company. Dating is just more work than I care to do at seventy-five."

"If I'm being honest, there's just not enough Black men our age available." Victoria downs another glass of wine.

Shirley rolls her eyes playfully. "Well, maybe you should broaden your horizons. You don't always have to date within your race."

"Yeah, I know that. I know we live in a very different time period. But when we were younger, we had to stick within our race unless we wanted to risk being killed. I grew up in

Mississippi, so you already know how that was. I don't know if I can just switch up now that it's acceptable."

"You know I never cared much about the outer appearance when it came to dating. Not that I had much experience back then. I just always knew that, whoever I fell in love with, I would love something deeper within them." I take a sip of the wine in front of me. "But I get it. For folks in our generation, it's not simply about preference. It was about survival. And it's hard to move past something that kept you alive."

There's a silent understanding amongst the group once I finish speaking. As I look around the table at the women sharing their stories of love and loss, I know we are all survivors of something or someone.

"I like this look on you, Peach." Roy appears across from me as if he's my spade's partner like he used to be.

"And what look is that?" I allow a sly smile to form.

"You know, confident. You look surer of yourself than I've seen in a long time. Like when we first met at that party and you barely gave me the time of day. That's how you look, but even more radiant."

"You know, I feel more confident. And don't get me wrong. I'm not always so sure of myself. Maybe I'm just becoming better at hiding it."

"If that's what it takes, then keep doing it."

"Why are you not angry, Roy? I've been dating a woman. Sleeping with her in our house. In our bed."

"Do you want me to be angry?"

"Yes, I do. Oh, I don't know. You just always had an opinion about everything, but now all you can talk about is how radiant I look."

"There's nothing else for me to talk about, Juliet. I'm not there. I can't control your life from the grave. I can't be upset with you about the life I'm not physically a part of anymore."

"But you're talking like you're not a part of my life at all."

"I'm not a part of your life right now. I'm a part of your past, your memories, the stories you tell. I'm not really here, Juliet."

My body heats up as if I've put my head into an oven. My hands shake, a shiver shoots up my spine, and sweat forms on the back of my neck and under my arms. Don't go back there, Juliet. You've been doing so well. You were having a good time tonight with the ladies. Don't go back to that dark place.

All I want to do is go home and crawl underneath my thick covers. I want to bury my body. My mind. Everything in my life has been going great. Why am I trying to sabotage my happiness with the sadness that lingers behind grief?

"Excuse me ladies, but I just got a slight headache that won't go away. I think I'm gonna call it a night." I excuse myself with goodbye hugs and surrender to the darkness I know is coming.

Chapter Seventeen

I CAN FEEL WINTER approaching, both inside my body and outside my door. I keep telling myself I don't want to go back to that dark hole I was in, but the more I try to run from it, the faster it catches up to me. I want to live in the light for as long as I possibly can. I want to continue to have the glow everyone keeps pointing out. I want to continue feeling like I'm floating when I walk. Have I not suffered enough? Isn't it time for me to be in the place in my life where everything is eternal bliss? If only Roy hadn't appeared at spades night. I wouldn't be in this funk where all I want to do is clean, watch the fire, and bury myself underneath my covers. Christmas is my favorite time of the year, and I haven't even thought about what I'm cooking, or what gifts I need to buy. I don't even have a wreath on the door. Time is moving fast, and here I am wholeheartedly believing I was moving along with it just fine. I close my eyes and tilt my head to the ceiling.

"I don't know what type of trick you're playing on me, but I need it to stop. I know I'm not the most religious person around, but those people sitting up there in their churches praising your name and cursing out their children and neighbors the next day can't be no better." Only in desperate times do I permit myself to speak aloud to the universe, to spirit, to God.

"You know I was dealt a pretty good hand. I had early success in a career that very few who look like me achieve. I have a beautiful daughter I am so proud of, grandchildren. I had a long marriage. I know what it feels like to love and be loved. And yet, for most of my life, I've felt guilty for having all of these things. I felt like I deserved none of them." I pace around the room as the sun starts to set.

"Don't I get a fucking break?"

Grief takes hold of me, and I sink to the couch in tears. Other than the crackling fire, everything is silent.

Somewhere in the silence I hear someone whisper, This is part of the plan. The voice doesn't sound like the burning bush in *The Ten Commandments* movie my family used to watch on Easter. This voice is softer, gentler. Mine. Out of nowhere, laughter catches me completely by surprise. I laugh until more tears come out of my eyes, then I cry until there's no more tears left. I walk into my room and pull out the yellow notepad I wrote my awakening plan in months ago. It feels like a lifetime ago, but there it is, marked with my birth date in ink. This is part of the plan, the heaviness, the tears. Sadness and anger are part of the adventure of grief.

"I don't know what to do anymore. I've done most of the things I sought out to do. I reawakened parts of myself I didn't know were asleep. Why does it feel like I'm back where I started? What am I supposed to do?" I toss my yellow notepad across the room. Maybe a shower will do me some good.

When I get out of the long hot shower, I collapse on my bed, exhausted by my own mind. My phone lights up and buzzes with a voice message from Destiny. My body doesn't want to lift a finger, but my mind keeps telling me to press play. Today the mind is apparently winning all battles.

"Hey Grandma, I wanted to stop by to tell you this in person, but I have a final exam and can't hold off on telling you. I think we found Ruby! I know you wanted me to stop looking, but I knew I would find her eventually. I mean she has zero online presence, so it was pretty hard. I did find this article from a couple of months ago about a retirement home in the town you grew up in with a picture of some of the residents. I'm gonna send you the picture. Let me know if it's her. Love you, Grandma, talk to you later."

My heart beats like a medicine drum, as I wait for the picture to load on my phone. It can't be her. It's probably someone else. I shouldn't get my hopes up. Nine times out of ten it's only going to lead to disappointment. The picture finally loads after what feels like the longest seconds of my life. A woman around the same age as me is sitting in a chair. I don't have to look too long to know that woman is Ruby. I know right away after seeing her eyes. My knees buckle, forcing me to sit down on the edge of my bed. I look at the frost and icicles hanging from my window. After the day I lashed out at Destiny for talking about Ruby, I was slowly giving up hope of ever finding her. I'd started to train my mind to become okay with the memories we shared so long ago.

After seeing her photo, my thoughts are no longer memories of the seventeen-year-old, twenty something, thirty-nine-year-old Ruby. I'm thinking of a Ruby whose skin is folded like mine, whose eyes have seen life. I know the retirement home she's in very well. I worked there right before I moved to California. How did Ruby end up there? How did she end up back in the one place she never wanted to return to? I look at the photo with teary eyes. I need to go home, to the first home I ever knew. After years away, I need to return to Georgia to see Ruby.

Chapter Eighteen

I BOOK A ONE-WAY flight to Georgia for the following week. But I have people to speak to before I fly off with no set return date. Elena is one of them. This year will be different for my family and friends. I'm never away for Christmas. Since my grandchildren were infants, they've been coming over to my house every year to open presents. I'll have a Christmas dinner this week and tell everyone my plans all at once. Except for Elena, she deserves a one-on-one.

"Hello, Elena."

"It's nice to hear your voice."

"It's nice to hear yours. Can we meet today for an impromptu date?"

"Sure, where to?"

"The fine arts museum at three."

"I look forward to seeing you."

My stomach feels like it just dropped to my feet. I don't want to hurt Elena. And to be honest, I don't want to leave her. These past few months with her have been the highlight of this journey, but she deserves to know about Ruby. She deserves to know that if there's the slightest chance I can spend the rest of my days with Ruby, I'm taking it.

We walk around the museum slowly. I'm savoring every second with Elena like the last drops of lemonade on a hot summer day.

"You're quiet today. What's on your mind?" she asks.

We're walking through the ceramics gallery, hand in hand.

"How about we take a seat." I walk over to a bench in the corner of an empty gallery. Elena follows behind me. Once we're both seated, I take her hands in mine.

"I care about you so much, Elena."

"Uh oh. This can't be good. There's someone else, isn't there?"

"Yes. Well no. Maybe. It's a little more complicated than that." I tell her everything about my birthday, the movie that sparked the memories, then finally Ruby. She listens quietly, never pulling her hands away from mine.

"I had a feeling something was pulling you elsewhere. I thought it was just because you had an artist's spirit. But a part of me wondered if it was someone else. You know, I've never had a love like you've described with Ruby. There's never been the one who got away, until now I suppose."

"Oh, Elena." Tears are waiting in my eyelids for their cue to exit. I knew this would be hard, but I didn't know it would feel like something being ripped from my body.

"It's okay. Our time together has been more than I could've imagined. I would be a hypocrite if I asked you to stay. I don't believe in living life with regrets. If our roles were reversed, I would do the same thing you're about to do. Of course, I wouldn't be as brave as you're being right now. But I'll be here when you get back, or whenever you need someone to talk to. I'm just a phone call away."

"Do you think I'm a horrible person who's been stringing you along for these past few months?"

"Not at all. You've never given me the impression you were stringing me along. I believe you were just as invested in our relationship as I was."

"I was."

"I know. I've fallen in love with you, Juliet. So as hard as it is to see you go, it would be harder to see you stay and be unhappy."

I pull her face close to mine and kiss her with all the passion a sad goodbye can handle. I pull away, leaving only our foreheads touching and our breath blending between us.

"I'm going to miss you, Elena."

She lifts my hand to her lips. "I'm going to miss you too, Juliet."

I lay my head on her shoulder and stare at Pablo Picasso's *Femme Assise* in front of us. The woman in the painting looks the way I feel at this moment. Somewhere within me is excitement that there's a chance I'll see Ruby again. But right now, all I can feel is sadness that this may be the last time I feel Elena's arms wrapped around me or feel her tattooed hand fit perfectly into mine. Over the past few months, Elena has become someone I can always turn to. She's received my seventy-five-year-old sensuality with open arms and an open heart. I've never had to pretend with her. She's never asked me to be anyone but Juliet. I sure hope finding Ruby is worth it, because I may be throwing away one of the best things to happen to me in years.

***

The impromptu Christmas dinner is scheduled for later this evening. Toni, Toni's husband Steven, Destiny, my grandson Luke, and Lili are all invited. It's going to be a family affair that's definitely needed after Destiny texted me yesterday. She slipped up and told her mom about my online dating. That explains why I haven't heard much from Toni. Usually, my phone is filled with messages of her checking in. Her recent messages have been dry, or there's been no messages at all. Honestly, not having her constantly check on me like I'm a ticking time bomb has been nice. But I want to be sensitive to her feelings. I'm still her mother, no matter how old she gets. I know that it's not always easy for children to see their parent in a new relationship. That's exactly why it's so important to have this dinner tonight.

My entire Sunday afternoon is filled with cooking and decorating the house with twinkling lights, Black Santas, and snowflakes Toni made when she was a child. The scent of pine from the Christmas tree I bought yesterday and the aromas from the kitchen are welcoming comforts. There's macaroni and cheese, collard greens, dressing, roasted chicken, rice and beans, and plenty of vegetables for Destiny, the only vegan in the family. The Temptations are singing "Silent Night," Otis Redding is telling me "Merry Christmas Baby," and of course, Eartha Kitt is making the possibility of meeting a very rich lover to buy anything I want to seem both sophisticated and alluring. I'm taking turns buzzing around the house and sitting on the couch with Roy to sing along to our favorite parts. The fire is dancing. The snow is inches high. The trees are resting, and the streets are quiet. My garden is mostly weeds. All the seeds are collected, the birds are sparse, and it's far too cold outside to sit on my porch and contemplate life.

I'm enjoying the warmth within my home. From tea, to fire, to warm bodies and warm conversations. Toni, on the other hand, is not prepared for the amount of change she sees as she walks through her childhood home.

"Wow, this place looks completely different, but cool. Not all boring like it used to be." Luke marvels at my once-hidden art pieces that are now on display.

"Luke, mind your manners," Steven scolds.

"Oh, that's quite all right. I'm glad you approve, Luke."

Toni silently walks around the house, observing. Judging. She seems completely annoyed by her son's enthusiasm over the changes I made without consulting her first.

"Now come give me hug. Before you know it, you're going to be taller than me!" I wrap my arms around Luke, who gives me a quick squeeze and makes a beeline toward the kitchen. He's straight up like a tree but can eat out a whole house. I make a note to keep an eye on him, so he doesn't go picking in all the food.

"Your place is really something, Juliet." Steven gives me a brief hug while looking around with an even more critical eye than Toni. It always surprises me how the two most straitlaced parents could produce some of the coolest children I know.

"I'm glad you like it, Steven."

His response is a simple grunt, as he hands me his thousand-dollar coat, a fact he manages to slide into conversation whenever he can. I gladly take that designer coat and throw it on the couch. Toni gives me a look I ignore. It's my house, meaning I can do whatever I want. I am not a maid to a man who thinks he's better than everyone in the family. Not too long ago, he didn't have a pot to piss in. He spent many nights on our couch when his parents kicked him out.

"It smells good in here!" Lili comes through the door with a bottle of wine in one hand and a dish in the other. Leave it to her to bring a dish to dinner, one that's guaranteed to be very tasty.

Lili gasps as she looks around. "I love it, Juli! All of it, the house, your dress, this glow that is blinding me right now."

"Thank you, Lili. I figured, since I'm already old, I might as well show off a little before it's too late." I shimmy in my red dress that has a slit up to my thigh.

"Cheers to that!" Lili says, as she raises the wine bottle.

Once Destiny and Trevor arrive, we all sit at the kitchen table to eat. Toni keeps looking at me as if I'm a thief amongst monks. It's clear she doesn't like the new look of the house, nor does she approve of how I'm dressed. I tap my knife against my glass to get everyone's attention.

"I want to thank everyone for coming. It means the world to me that I can have all of those I love sitting together at this table. I've been cooking all day, so I truly hope you all enjoy it. Dig in!" Plates clatter as hands unwrap the foil and scoop out their portions. Toni keeps glaring at me.

"I want to know who this stranger is sitting at our table." Toni's voice silences the entire room in less than a second, which is the exact response she's hoping for. Always one for the dramatics.

"And who's the stranger?" I continue to fix my plate.

"You."

"Oh, I see. So you want to know why I'm sitting at *my* table?"

"I want to know what we're doing here. It's not Christmas, so why are we having a Christmas dinner? And why are you dressed like that? I can see your entire thigh. Most importantly, when were you going to tell us you're going on blind dates?"

"I guess I can start with the first question. I wanted everyone to come here tonight because I won't be here for Christmas."

"Where are you going?" Luke asks with a mouth full of macaroni and cheese.

"I'm going to go visit someone in Georgia, and I don't know how long I'll be gone. But I do know that I won't be here for the holidays."

"We always have Christmas here," Toni says.

"This year we're not. Now to answer your next question, I'm wearing this dress because I like it, and I look damn good in it. Especially my legs."

"I agree." Lili downs her second cup of eggnog.

"As for the final, and apparently most important, question about the blind dates I went on...well, it was none of your business. Besides, it doesn't matter now. I haven't been on a blind date in quite some time because I've taken on a lover. Her name is Elena. Or at least I had a lover whose name is Elena."

A piece of chicken falls out of Luke's hand. "Should I be here for this?"

"Quiet, Luke." Destiny kicks him under the table.

Toni's breath visibly speeds up, and she grabs hold of the side of her chair to remain stable. Lili tries to hide her smile.

Steven almost chokes on his water. Destiny snickers, which is something she always does in awkward situations. The only sound in the room is the soft Christmas music and Trevor, the new boyfriend, clinking his fork on the plate as he continues eating, oblivious to what's happening around him.

"Are there any questions?" I meet everyone's eyes.

"You're dating a woman, Grandma?" Luke asks.

"Yes."

"Since when do you date women?" Toni jumps in after shushing Luke.

"Well actually, since I was a teenager."

"Who are you going to meet in Georgia?" Toni asks.

"If you must know, I'm going to see one of the loves of my life. Her name is Ruby. We grew up together there."

"Ruby. Love of your life?" Toni voice is dripping in disgust.

"Yes."

"I thought Daddy was the love of your life."

"He was one of them. The other was Ruby." I take a sip of the eggnog in front of me.

"Did Daddy know about her?"

"No, I never got the chance to tell him."

"So that's how you're going to replace him? That's how you're going to honor my father's legacy, by having a random *woman* in his bed! And going off to see *another* woman you claim was the love of your life that no one has ever heard of until tonight!"

"Mom, relax. You're getting worked up over nothing." Destiny jumps to my defense.

"I am relaxed, Destiny. I'm just asking simple questions. This does involve us, after all. Right, Mom?" Toni looks at me with combative eyes that remind me of when she was a teenager. I feel a gentle smile growing on my face. I wasn't fazed back then, and I'm not fazed now. I calmly run my hand over my thigh to smooth out any wrinkles on my dress and look up, so my gaze is steady on hers. "No one can ever replace your father. But he's no longer here, and I'm no longer wasting my days until I can join him wherever he is. So yes, I do share my bed with a lovely woman whom I deeply care for. And yes, I am going to see another woman who I have loved my entire life. But do understand that none of it is to dishonor your father. All of it's to honor me."

Toni is silent. Her gaze moves from me to the new additions around her childhood home, then to everyone at the table holding their breaths, waiting for whatever she has to say next.

"Why tell us anything that's been going on in your life? Why even invite us over here? You've been making decisions without any of us in mind since your birthday. From redecorating your house, to getting rid of Daddy's things, to dating. Nothing had to change. You could've gone on living the life you're living, while we remained in ignorant bliss."

"And have you all been living blissfully? Because on my end, I see a daughter who worries to the point where she's one step away from handing me brochures for a retirement home." I take a bite of pie on my plate. Instead of my favorite sweet potato, my tongue only tastes something bitter. My appetite is now nonexistent, and I'm growing tired of the conversation, of explaining myself.

"She wouldn't do that, Grandma." Destiny looks at her mother for confirmation.

"Stay out of this, Destiny. This doesn't concern you."

"Mom, this doesn't concern you either. It's Grandma's life, not yours." Destiny stares at her mother with the same steadfast eyes. Toni pushes her chair back from the table.

"Well done, Mom. It looks like everyone agrees with you living your life without including any of us in it. So I'm just going to leave and let you all get back to this dinner. Steven, Luke grab your coats and let's go."

I place a piece of foil over Luke's plate for him to take to go.

"Sorry, Grandma." Luke hugs me and kisses me on the cheek.

"Don't you worry about that. I've known your mother a long time. I birthed her. She'll get over it. Now don't forget to check underneath the tree for your gift." I give him a wink and send him on his way. The dining room is quiet except for the music in the background and the occasional car passing by on the icy streets.

"I say if Elena and Ruby make you happy, then who cares what anyone thinks. To hell with them!" Lili lifts her glass of eggnog and Destiny lifts hers as well.

"I second that!"

"Thank you. I really appreciate it."

I pack leftovers for the hungry college students and send everyone home with hugs and kisses and their still-wrapped gifts. I tend to the fire, then sit on the couch with a full belly and heavy heart. Only firelight and a few candles chase any shadows from the room. I steep a cup of lavender and chamomile tea, then join Roy, who was here on the couch throughout the entire dinner.

"I can tell by how your skin is folded between your eyebrows that you're still bothered by Toni's outburst. But tonight, we're not going to talk about Toni. We've spent many nights in front of this fireplace talking about our daughter."

Roy stands up and holds out his hand. "Would you like to dance with me, Ms. Juliet?"

I'm so deep in my thoughts that when I look up and see Roy's face and his beautiful, gapped-tooth smile, I forget he's not actually here. How many times has he asked me to dance in front of the fire on a cold night? Too many times for me to remember. I blink away tears and take his hand. We slow dance to Nat King Cole. I forget about time when I'm dancing. When my body sways to a rhythm, I'm no longer Juliet. I have no worries, no fears. The dance is moving through me as effortlessly as the wind moves through a bird taking flight. My thoughts of Toni disappear as my feet shuffle from side to side. I look into Roy's eyes and see the simplest form of love. Love isn't only for the young. I've lived long enough to know that real love resides underneath the flowers, kisses, chocolates, and words of affection. Real love is in the listening ear, or a shoulder to cry on. It's in the meals cooked, the gentle reminders, apologies, and the silent moments. Love is a practice. Love is devotion.

"You know, I still can't believe you went out dancing with Destiny."

"Me neither. I don't know what I did that night, but my body is still recovering months later. I may never be the same." We both laugh softly.

"Remember that club we went to that was supposed to be for a mature crowd? We were what fifty-five give or take."

I scrunch up my nose as I think about it. "Yeah, it was a little too old and stuffy for my taste."

"With your track record, I bet it was."

We continue to laugh and talk about nothing in particular. When it's time to go to bed, I lay awake, thinking of how grateful I am for the shadow of loneliness not hanging over me like it used to. I know, very well, how quickly life can change. So I stare at the ceiling and count my blessings until I fall asleep.

Chapter Nineteen

I'M SITTING IN THE car, fidgeting with the ends of my scarf, as Destiny drives me to the airport.

"What are your plans for when you land?" Destiny asks.

"Plans? What type of plans?"

"You know, like are you gonna go and find Ruby right away or are you gonna take some time, maybe some days, to ground and then go find her."

I haven't thought about what I'm going to do once I get there. "I don't know." I start to laugh. "I don't even know where I'm going to stay."

"Grandma, that's not okay. Your flight leaves in a couple of hours. I can't just drop you off without you having a place to stay."

"Oh, don't you worry about me. I'll find a place. I'll be fine."

"You know, for someone who loves planning her life out, this is really unlike you. And it's kinda irresponsible."

"It is, isn't it." I grin.

I'm still smiling and laughing softly to myself as I board the plane. I'm nervous and giddy. I haven't been to my hometown since my father died almost twenty years ago. Last I heard, Creekstone has turned into a sort of ghost town where the only thing one can do is sit around and wait for death. There are times when I miss the red dirt that got on all my nice clothes. I miss the smell of the country rain and the humid air that gave my skin a naturally youthful glow. The yearlong sunshine was only hidden during the rainy season. There hasn't been anything in Creekstone for me in a long time. Now there's the possibility of Ruby. I wonder what she's like now. Has life been kind to her? I hope so. I wonder if she has the same laugh. I wonder if she'll even want to see me.

I tighten the scarf around my neck, as I step out of the car I took from the airport. I pause a moment to soak in my surroundings, the land and trees. I study the old houses, some occupied, some abandoned. The smell of something fried is coming from a local restaurant not too far from where I'm standing. A wave of knowing washes over me. My body knows every inch of this town. It remembers the faint smell of white pine being cut for the winter months, and the sight of blossoming dogwood trees in spring. My hands will never forget the feeling of digging up sassafras roots in the woods whenever someone we knew had an upset stomach. I still remember, by name, the various bird songs in this region. Although I left here believing I would never return, this town has never left me. Now here I am, nervous and also excited about what could be. With my one suitcase, I head toward a local bed-and-breakfast that has been here since I was a teenager. I made the reservation right before I left the airport.

News travels fast that I'm back home. People can't believe it. I'm kind of a local celebrity, even though most of the people here have never seen one of my paintings. All they know, thanks to my father who bragged about me all the time, is that I'm a world-famous artist. Someone who grew up here, got out, and made something of herself. Even as I roll my suitcase to the bed-and-breakfast, strangers are already coming up to welcome my arrival. My least favorite thing about living in a small town was always that your business is everybody's business.

"Ms. Juliet, it is so good to see you!" I don't know who the young woman is, but I don't want to be rude. Her name tag says Regina.

"It's good to see you too, Regina."

"How was your trip? It's surprising to see you here after all these years."

I can tell she wants to say more. I'm sure she wants to know what I've been up to for the past twenty years, and why I came back to town. Most likely so she can tell her family and friends, who I'm sure are waiting patiently for any information. My lips are as sealed as my suitcase.

"It's been a long trip, and I've been thinking about how good it's gonna feel when I lay my head on a pillow since I boarded the plane."

Regina turns to grab my room key off the wall behind her. "Understood. We can catch up later. My dad is really looking forward to seeing you."

I take the keys and smile. "I look forward to seeing him as well. Take care now."

***

After a very restful night, I make my way down to the dining area for breakfast.

"Juliet Livingston! It's been a long time since I've said a name so sweet."

I turn to find one of my dearest childhood friends standing behind me. I was so tired yesterday that I completely forgot this bed-and-breakfast is owned by his family. Now it makes since why Regina spoke to me as if she knew me. She's Theodore's daughter. I don't believe I've seen her since she was a little girl.

"Theodore, still a smooth talker I see."

"I can't believe you're here. How long has it been?"

"Too long to remember. How are you?"

"Oh fine, considering. Just running this old place with my daughter." Theodore sits next to me at the table.

"I can't believe how grown-up she is. I didn't even recognize her."

"Time flies."

I pick around the eggs on my plate, thinking of our childhood days together. Theodore lowers his voice and leans in closer. "So tell me, why are you really here?"

"I don't know what you mean."

"Come on, Juliet. After all these years, you just wanted to come back and walk around town."

"Maybe I missed Creekstone."

"And maybe you're lying."

I drop my napkin on top of my food and scoot my chair away from the table. "Look, I didn't come to breakfast to be antagonized and have you in my business."

"I don't mean to antagonize you. I just remember that, out of everyone in this town, two people were adamant about leaving this place and never coming back. That was you and Ruby. Now, Ruby made her way back here decades ago. I'm just curious about what brought you back suddenly."

I freeze hearing Theodore mention Ruby. I hope it's not written all over my face, but I know how easy it always was for him to tell if I was hiding something. He was my only guy friend, and everyone thought we should date in high school, including him. Eventually, he found out about my feelings for

Ruby. Even now, I can see the wheels turning in his head as he puts pieces together just by looking at my face. He should've been a detective. He's a walking lie detector.

"You came back for Ruby, didn't you?"

I don't answer. I just grab my bag to head for the door.

"I think it'll be best if I find other living arrangements."

"Oh come on now, Juls. You know I wouldn't tell anybody. You see I haven't after half a century." He pulls gently on my arm. I sit back down at the table, and Theodore brings me a fresh cup of green tea.

"How long have you known she's back in town?"

"I just found out last week."

"When was the last time you two spoke?"

"Thirty something years ago."

"You know where she is, don't you?"

"At the retirement community, if I'm not mistaken."

"You're not. She's been there for years."

Years. For years Ruby has been back in our childhood town. I wonder if she ever thought about reaching out. Wouldn't being back in the place of our young love stir up memories? It does for me. Too many memories to be exact.

"Have you seen her?" I ask.

"Occasionally. Folks at the center usually stay pretty cooped up in that place. They have everything they need, so there's no reason for them to leave unless they really want to."

"How does she look?"

He shrugs. "Like Ruby, pretty as always."

Should I go to the center right this moment and see Ruby for myself or wait? Why are you such a chicken, Juliet? Theodore has confirmed she's alive. I've had thoughts of the long speech I would give her if I visited her grave. I imagined the tears I would cry and the flowers I would bring. My imagination hasn't prepared me for the reality of Ruby being alive.

"Are you all right? You look a little pale." Theodore offers me a glass of water.

"I think I just need to lie down."

"Oh no you don't. You're not gonna go back up to that room and talk yourself out of going to see Ruby. Come on. We'll take a walk and get some fresh air." I always hated how much Theodore could read me like a book. He used to know me so well that I would always say if Roy hadn't come into the picture, he would've probably been my husband.

"Fine. But just for a little while. I don't want folks to get the wrong idea and start gossiping about how they think we're dating." I give Theodore a little push and grab my sweater.

"You know you would have to get in line, right?"

"Is that right?"

"Yeah, that's right."

We walk out the door and catch up, or in my case, I walk out the door and distract myself for a little longer.

Chapter Twenty

RED AND GREEN GARLANDS wrap around the streetlights lining the quiet road. Lawn decorations wait until nightfall to show off all their twinkling glory. I'm watching a small woman clean the nativity scene in front of the only church in town, only days before Christmas. My heart aches as I wander down roads, around corners, and into buildings of my childhood. Some sort of muscle memory leads me to the one place I thought I would never go back to. The home me, my father, and my mother once shared as a family looks run-down and aged, yet still the same. Homes were built to last during those times. This small home was built by my father and some of the other men in town. The grass is overgrown with weeds. Vines are overtaking the house. The windows are boarded up, and the front steps are broken. Other than that, the house is still standing.

I stop a man walking past. "Excuse me."

He removes his earphones. "Yeah?"

"Do you live near here?"

"Not too far."

"Do you know, by chance, if anyone has lived here in a while?"

The man smirks and scratches his beard. "Nah, no one will go near that house. It's giving me the creeps just standing in front of it."

"What do you mean?"

"Everybody in this town knows that house is haunted. Been that way as long as I remember, and I've lived here my entire life."

"I could've sworn someone was living there at one point."

"Not as far as I know. My grandma used to say that there was a young couple who went to take a look at the house and ran right back out when they heard a voice inside telling them they'll kill their firstborn child. Now, I don't know how true all of it is. But the rumors stuck."

I can tell the man is getting antsy with every passing second, but I have to ask one last question.

"So how come the city hasn't torn it down?"

"I told you, lady. Nobody wants to go near that house. Besides, nobody cares about this town, let alone that house. There are so many abandoned houses around, you kinda forget they're here."

He walks off, leaving me staring at the house and knowing exactly who's doing the haunting.

I find myself in Toasty's Diner for lunch. My appetite has been up and down these past few days, but I'm craving their famous grilled cheese. I used to save my money to eat here. Me and Ruby would babysit for multiple families in a week, just so we could split the jumbo grilled cheese at the diner. The best times were when we saved up enough money to take some home with us. I would always save half for my mother, who would come back from her weekend binges smelling of alcohol, hungry and hungover. Just for a second, she would pat me on the head and say, "Good girl, you knew your momma needed this."

It was a brief and futile compliment, but I would carry those two words to bed with me as if they were a good-night hug.

"You do know they have other things on their menu, Peach?"

Roy sits across from me as he used to when we came to town. He leans back, with a toothpick dangling out the corner of his mouth and a smile that challenges everything in sight.

"I know but why try something new when I can stick with what I know is good."

"Yeah, but wasn't the whole point of that plan of yours to add some excitement in your life? Be fearless?"

"How does not eating a grilled cheese sandwich make me fearless?"

"Sometimes it's the small things, Peach. Just because you're back in your hometown doesn't mean you have to go backward."

He disappears just as fast as he appeared, when the waitress lays a menu on the table.

"Hey, aren't you Juliet, that famous painter?"

"Yes, that's me," I stammer, as my mind tries to process what Roy just said.

Backward. If anything, I feel as if I'm going forward at full speed with no stop sign in sight.

"Wow, everyone's been talking about you, and here you are right in front of me during my shift. And to think I was gonna call in sick."

The young girl, who looks around Destiny's age, sits down in front of me. Finally coming back to the present moment, I smile at how excited the girl is to meet me.

"Well it seems you know my name, but I don't know yours."

"Oh right, of course. I'm Winnie."

"It's nice to meet you, Winnie."

"I know this might seem strange, but I just have to spit it out and say that you're such an inspiration. You grew up in the same town I did and got out and became an artist. I want to become a documentary photographer, but my parents don't support it. Not to mention I just found out I'm pregnant, and of course, the father wants nothing to do with me or our future child. I am double screwed, and my life feels like it's over, and I'm sorry if that was a lot. Sometimes, when I'm nervous, I just vomit up words."

"There's no need to be nervous. I'm just a person. Also, life doesn't end just because you have a child, if you choose to have the child."

"You know what's even crazier, Ms. Juliet?"

"What's that, Winnie?"

"I always pictured myself going to these far-off lands with a baby on my back and a camera in hand, taking pictures for big magazines."

"Perhaps you were getting a glimpse into your future."

Winnie leans back in the booth and places her hand on her belly that has not yet expanded. "I don't know. I can't afford college. I'm working myself to the bone to save money to get out of here and go to a city where art is appreciated. But every passing day, that picture of my future is fading."

I'm staring at a younger version of myself. I wasn't pregnant when I left, but I still had a dream of leaving behind the home I knew and the person I once was, to reinvent myself as an artist somewhere far away.

"How old are you, Winnie?"

"Nineteen."

"If I could do it all over again, I would take more risks sooner. I would believe in myself and my talent, even if I hadn't landed that dream job yet. I would believe in myself so much that I'd submit some of my paintings to a contest and maybe win a one-way flight to Paris. That's where I wanted to go at your age. Where do you want to go, Winnie? Where's the place where you think your artist's heart will soar?"

A slow smile spreads across Winnie's face as she leans closer. "Brazil. I've always wanted to go to Brazil."

"Brazil is beautiful, vibrant, and full of life. You go to Brazil, you and your baby, and become the best documentary photographer you can be."

"But what about my parents?"

"What about them?"

"It'll be hard, you know, without their support. I don't have a camera besides my phone. My child won't have a father, and I'll be completely alone."

"You won't be alone. Someone is waiting inside you that only wants you to be happy. Because if you're happy, they're happy. As for your child not having a father, that doesn't matter as long as they have you. Life will be challenging, but usually, the things that are worth it take a lot more effort and time to get there. The things that are challenging are far more rewarding."

Winnie gets up and hugs me. How I've become the advice-giver to young people these last few months is beside me. I guess I've lived long enough to know a thing or two.

"Oh I forgot to get your order. Do you need time to look over the menu some more?"

I think about it for a second and decide to take all of the go-for-it and be-courageous advice I've been giving out. I hand Winnie the menu. "You can just bring out two orders of your favorite thing on the menu. I would love to hear more about how you got into photography. If you don't mind joining me for lunch."

Winnie's eyes widen with excitement, and she hurries back to the kitchen to place the order. In ten minutes, two jumbo, grilled cheese sandwiches are sitting in front of me. As I bite into the familiar warm and gooey sandwich in front of me, I catch Roy in the corner of my eye, laughing and shaking his head. If not for Winnie, I would have laughed out loud too.

Chapter Twenty-One

MY LIFE HAS ALWAYS been full of secrets. I remember the first secret I ever kept. I was six and too sick to go to school. My momma volunteered to stay home with me to help me get well. She gave me soup and tucked me into bed. On my way to the bathroom, I caught her taking a wad of money out from underneath the mattress. My father kept money there, saving to buy us a new house. I couldn't understand why she was taking the money. A creaky floorboard made my presence known, and she almost jumped out of her skin. She whipped around to look at me. I knew I was watching her do something she wasn't supposed to. She rushed over and bent down to my level.

"You 'bout gave me a heart attack, sneakin' up on me like that. What are you doin' out of bed?"

"I needed to go to the bathroom," I mumbled, still moving in and out of my fever. "Why did you take that money from under the mattress? Are we about to get a new house?"

She smoothed down my hair with her hand, something she only did when she needed a favor from me. "No, we're not gettin' a new house. I need some money for some things, but you can't tell Daddy. I wanna surprise him."

"You're gettin' him a gift?"

"Yeah, I'm gettin' him a gift. But it's gotta be our little secret."

I promised to keep the secret and was sent back to my room. From my small bedroom window overlooking the front of the house, I saw Momma give the wad of money to some man I had seen a few times in the neighborhood. I remember kids in the neighborhood saying that if you wanted to find out something that was hidden, he was the man to go to. I didn't know what they meant by that at the time. All I knew was that he wore an expensive-looking suit with a cigarette tucked behind his ear, and people were always giving him money. Even though I didn't know she was paying that man to confirm whether or not my father was cheating, I knew for certain that money wasn't to get my daddy a gift.

My father wasn't a saint either. I kept his secret when I caught him cheating on Momma with my soon-to-be stepmom. I was seven years old, still wearing knee-high socks and riding my green bike to the store with Ruby to buy penny candy. Right as we were walking out the corner store, I heard a deep and boisterous laugh I would know anywhere. My head spun toward that laugh. I had to squint against the blinding sun for a few seconds to see a woman with her arm wrapped around my father's neck. They were between two buildings, hidden from anyone who didn't know that laugh. I dropped my brown paper bag full of candy and walked across the street.

"Juliet, where are you goin?" Ruby grabbed my bag of candy and ran after me.

"You're gonna get hit by a car walking that slow across the street." Just as Ruby called out, a car honked its horn and swerved around both of us. My father locked eyes with me. He ran out from the shadows and into the street with his usual look of a concerned parent. I was confused by his concern. He looked like my father, sounded like my father. But my father was supposed to be at work, not in an alley with a strange woman. He pulled me and Ruby out of the street and onto the sidewalk.

"What are you two doing out in the middle of the road? You could've been killed!"

Although his hands were on my shoulders, I was staring at the woman.

"What were you doin' with her?" I looked into my father's eyes. He was one of my favorite people in the world. He wouldn't lie to me, but he might not tell me the whole truth, since I was a child and all.

"I can't tell you that yet. You'll find out soon enough, suga plum. In the meantime, you can't tell your momma what you saw here. Okay?" Another secret to keep, just like my mother giving money to that man. My stomach churned. That's when I realized I hated secrets. I promised myself that, when I got older, I wouldn't have any.

"Okay," I told him.

"Good girl."

I didn't keep that promise to my seven-year-old self. Life continued to happen, and I had a little more understanding of why adults kept things hidden the way they did. I couldn't tell people I was in love with my best friend, Ruby. I couldn't tell Roy that I was even more like my father than I realized after cheating on him with Ruby. I could never tell Toni that there were moments when I felt so alone that all I wanted to do was leave her with her father and run off into the mountains to paint in peace and live freely. No, I didn't tell any of my secrets. I became the gatekeeper of all that was meant to remain hidden. I accepted my role and thought I had moved on with my life. But I didn't move on. The hidden lives within me are simply gnawing their way through my body. Eventually, they'll consume me whole.

After tormenting myself for several hours, I finally got to sleep in the morning's early hours, only to be woken up by birdsong. If I had a rock in my hand, I might throw it at them just to get them to fly away and leave me alone. Instead of my usual tea, I drink a sip of black coffee to help get me going.

"Well good morning, sunshine!" Theodore comes into the dining room just as chirpy as the birds outside my window. I'm tempted to throw a rock at him as well.

"You look like hell. Is your bed not comfortable enough for you?" He sits down at the table and pours himself a cup of coffee.

"The bed's fine. I just had a lot on my mind, that's all."

"I see. I'm about to go on my morning walk. Care to join me?"

"Walking requires more energy than I have."

"It may help to clear your head. The sun's shining, breeze's blowing, and birds are chirping."

"Don't remind me about the birds." We grab our coats and head for the outside world.

The cool air helps to organize my thoughts. Unfortunately, nothing is clearing out. I still know this woods trail by heart, even though I haven't walked down it since I was a teenager. Watching my feet walk along the familiar soil and dying leaves startles me, like I've been transported back in time and am on my way to meet Ruby at our secret spot. I look up to see the lake, still shimmering.

"Did you bring me here on purpose?"

"Actually, I was following you." Theodore sits on one of the benches. I feel both betrayed and impressed by my body's memory. I hadn't planned on coming here to the lake in the same way I hadn't planned on going to see my old house. I sit beside Theodore and gaze out at the dock on the other side of the lake. It looks smaller than I remembered.

"I'm surprised that dock hasn't rotted away by now."

"I'm surprised this whole town hasn't rotted away, yet here we are."

"I haven't been here since I was practically a child. That day, I told Ruby I couldn't go with her to college." I readjust the green knitted scarf around my neck, as the memory of that day replays in my mind.

"How's it feels to be back?"

"It feels like I never left. When I got into town on the first day, it felt like time was frozen. The only thing that got older was me. But being back here at the lake makes me feel like a teenager again.

"You know, me and Ruby used to go skinny-dipping here during the full moon. It became our tradition." The memory softens my face into a wistful smile.

Theodore chuckles. "I knew you were a wild one, just by the way you used to walk in those Daisy Dukes. You knew exactly what you were doing."

"Oh please, I was no wilder than you were. How many girlfriends did you have at the same time, five?"

"Hey this isn't about me."

"Then who's it about?"

"It's about you and Ruby. You've been in town a couple of days now and still haven't seen her. How come?"

"I'm afraid she won't want to see me. The last time we saw each other ended on a pretty bad note."

"You didn't come all this way to sit at the lake and take walks with me. You came here for her."

"I know! You don't have to remind me of the reason I'm here."

"You sure about that?"

I look back out at the lake, at the sun weaving through the ripples.

"You're right. I'm wasting time. I should go see her even if she doesn't want anything to do with me."

"Try not to go in there with fear. You never know what can happen."

I stand and kiss Theodore on the cheek.

"Wait, you're going right now?"

"I need to make a quick stop first. But I'm going right after! Thank you, Theodore."

I walk to my childhood home and actually step inside. The only light is coming from the open door and gaps in the boarded-up windows. There are spiderwebs and rat droppings everywhere. The pipes have been stolen. Broken glass lays in piles on the floor, and it smells like mildew.

As my eyes adjust to the faint light, I can see not much has changed. Everything is just old, torn, or worn down. Something falls behind me. I turn around slowly, not sure what I may find. What I do see catches me off guard far more than a family of rats would. A cigarette dangles from the mouth of a woman wearing a purple housecoat, who's sitting in a broken chair. Her face is a mirror of mine.

"You think you can just come into my house uninvited."

"I'm not sure there was any way for you to stop me," I say with a trembling voice.

"What did you say to me, girl?"

"With all due respect, Momma, I'm not a girl. I've surpassed that stage in my life."

"Is that right? Now you some uppity artist, comin' down here to slum it with the folks you left behind."

I remain silent, trying to hold onto my composure, my peace. I haven't seen my mother in this form for a long time. It brings up long nights of waking in a sweat next to Roy as nightmare after nightmare played through my dreams, always starring the one and only mommy dearest.

"What girl, a cat got your tongue? Oh nah, I know exactly why you're here. You're here to see that blue-eyed girl."

"You know her name is Ruby. You knew her from when she was a little girl. You were friends with her mother!"

"I don't know that bulldagger in the same way I don't know you!"

I look around the abandoned house that's crumbling before my eyes. After my mother found out about me and Ruby, she called us bulldaggers until she decided not to utter another word to me, up to her death. It was always a silly word, old school and meaningless to my ears. My mother spit it out as if she were throwing a knife straight into my heart. The word itself never hurt me, but the hate behind it always did. Standing here in what was once the living room, I feel as if I'm shrinking like Alice after she drank the potion. I'm reverting to a young girl who wished desperately to jump into a hole and be transported to a new world. To safety. I listen to my mother's verbal attacks with a young heart and closed lips.

"You think you can come into my house! I didn't leave it to you for a reason. Why, so you and that girl could be laying all up with each other under my roof!

"I raised you in the church, and you turned out just as ugly as the devil himself! And I blame your father. If he didn't leave, you wouldn't have ever been with that girl!

"And you thought you could save yourself by marrying a man. Ha! God remembers everything. He remembers everything!

"You and that blue-eyed girl gonna rot in hell!"

The attacks keep coming. Eventually, I tune her out to protect my sanity. I look around the house once more, and at my mother who's still seated in the corner. She always sat there with a cigarette hanging out of her mouth, waiting for my father to return home from work, then waiting to yell at him for coming home so late. When they finally separated, she sat there to watch what was going on in the neighborhood so she could gossip with the other women.

"You were lonely," I whisper in a voice that belongs to my seven-year-old self.

"Excuse me!"

"You were lonely and bitter." My voice strengthens and deepens as I grow into my teenage self. "It wasn't me you were angry at. It was the fact that I reminded you of him and that you knew he was my favorite."

"I ought to slap the black off you, talkin' to me like that!"

"But you can't because you're no longer here."

My mother sits back in the chair, eyes filled with disbelief.

I'm an adult woman, a mother, and wife. "You resented me because he didn't leave me. He left you. If he were like some of those other men who leave their wives and families and never look back, you would have never treated me the way you did. Because I would've been abandoned like you."

I age back into my seventy-five-year-old self with every step closer to my mother.

"I didn't abandon you, even when I probably should've."

I kneel until I'm at eye level with the woman who birthed me.

"I was the one you treated the worst. I'm the reason why you're still here, reliving all that happened in this house, day in and day out. I was the one who was with you until you took your last breath. Me, Momma! Your daughter."

My mother turns her head to the window.

"It's okay. You don't have to look at me. You don't have to admit or apologize for the pain you inflicted on the only person who never left you. I didn't realize how much I was holding onto that wound you dug your knife so deeply into. I can't hold onto it any longer. I blamed you for so much. I blamed you for me not being with Ruby. I blamed you for me not going to college. I blamed you for the sadness that's always lingering inside of me. But I'm done blaming you.

"Momma, I love you. And I know somewhere behind your hurt and your pain is a mother who loves me too. For that reason alone, I forgive you."

My mother's head whips back around to look at me. She looks so lifelike that I want to reach out and touch her cheek as I do with Toni and my grandchildren. I'm no longer looking at the woman who haunted me, abused me, shaped me into the woman I am. I see the woman who would swoop me into her arms as we danced to her soft humming. She's the woman who allowed me to lick the icing off the spoon after she was done making her special buttercream cake for the community Bake-Off. This is the woman who made up elaborate bedtime stories with the eloquence of a seasoned storyteller, as I nestled into her rhythmic belly and fell asleep. In front of me is a mother who was once filled with softness, but who didn't know how to cope after being hurt by the love of her life. I know what it feels like to lose the one you love. Instead of getting angry and taking it out on the world, I became a recluse and hid from the world around me. We both ran away from grief. We both had our ways of coping. I guess I'm more like her than I thought. Whether I want to be or not, I am my mother's daughter.

I close my eyes and whisper, "I'm letting you go now."

I expect to hear a loud explosion from the sky or to see a light shining down from the heavens. I expect to experience some sort of supernatural event like the ones I was taught in Sunday school. There's just silence. When I open my eyes, my mother is gone.

I get up slowly from my knees and take one last look at my childhood home. There is nothing left for me here. Nothing but ashes, dust, and old memories. I walk out the door feeling lighter than when I walked in. I won't be returning here again.

As I walk down the stairs, a bird lands just in front of me. The red cardinal is associated with angels, spirit guides, and ancestors. My mother is telling me the one thing I always wanted to hear, "Thank you."

***

Do clouds feel like this after releasing all their rain? I've never felt so clear in my life, not even when I was standing naked in front of that mirror. That was only the beginning. By the time I make it to the retirement community, my hands are freezing from the sudden drop in temperature. Thank goodness I have my scarf and an extra pair of mittens in my bag. The entrance to the retirement center is just as I remembered. Gold chandeliers, fresh flowers in expensive glass vases, paintings, and sculptures transport me to the fanciest hotel somewhere in a big city. The only changes are the faces of the older people moving about. They used to be all white. The only people of color in the building were the staff. Now there's a mixture. Times have changed.

Here I am, standing at the front desk where I worked right before I left.

"Hi, my name's Amber. Can I help you with somethin', ma'am?" A young, white girl who resembles a younger Dolly Parton stands behind the desk with a wide grin.

"I'm looking for a woman who lives here."

"I can help you with that. What's her name? I'll type it in to see if she's accepting visitors."

"Her name is Ruby, but I actually don't know if her last name has changed since I last saw her."

"That's okay. How does she look? I know everyone around here."

I pause to think. The only recent image of Ruby I can go off of is the one Destiny sent me. She looked as I remember her. "She has dark-brown skin and blue eyes."

"Say no more! I know exactly who you're looking for! Ms. Ruby, she's the sweetest. No one ever comes to visit her. She'll be so happy. Can I get your name so I can tell her you're here to see her?"

"Juliet."

"Okay, Ms. Juliet, I'll just be one moment."

The young girl practically skips off to go tell Ruby. That's when my nerves finally hit. They start in my feet, which prevents me from keeping still. Then they move up to my stomach, causing bubbles to take over and my gut to tighten. They move past my heart quickly since it doesn't take long for it to start beating faster. Until they make it to their true destination. What if I came all this way, and she doesn't want to see me? What did I do all of this for? I shouldn't have come here. It was a stupid, stupid thing to do!

"Ms. Juliet."

I turn to face the girl, bracing myself for the worst.

"She's ready to see you now."

Chapter Twenty-Two

GOLD CASING TRIMS THE borders of this long, white hallway's walls. Welcome mats of all shapes and sizes sit cozily in front of each door, and holiday decorations make the passageway jovial and inviting. I smell fresh, white laundry, cookies, and floral perfume. Looks like they're having a party. It's truly a retirement community, like Spring Oaks back home. Residents peek out of their rooms as I pass. They probably think I'm a new resident.

Room 233. Before I can build up the nerves to knock, a soft voice behind the door says, "Come in."

Ruby. It's her voice. After all these years, I would recognize her voice anywhere.

I slowly open the door and see Ruby sitting in a green armchair. Pressed, grey hair reaches just to the shoulders of her powder-blue sweater. I notice her white pants, white top, white nursing shoes, and a pearl necklace.

"Juliet, is that really you?"

I don't say anything for a while. I stand in the entrance with the door wide open behind me and study Ruby. I'm really here, standing in front of the first person I loved and kept loving for most of my life. How many people can say that? How many people *want* to say it? My nerves haven't settled yet, and it's taking all of my inner strength to not bolt in the opposite direction. This is a mistake! A huge mistake! Abort mission, Juliet! Abort mission!

"Can you close the door behind you? Some of these folks are the nosiest people I've ever been around."

I snap out of my daze and quickly close the door behind me. The apartment is dimly lit. Christmas lights twinkle across a large window overlooking the silhouettes of trees. I don't know what to say. I haven't fully thought about what it would be like to be in front of Ruby again. Sometimes I daydreamed about a grand reunion where we would run into each other's arms for a long and warm embrace. Other times I imagined Ruby would still be holding a grudge for kicking her out of my room back in Ireland. I imagined her cursing me out and throwing things and being as dramatic as when we were younger. Ruby just sits there. I'm a little underwhelmed and disappointed. I expected more. Perhaps I wanted more.

"Did something happen to your voice?" Ruby teases.

I clear my throat. "No, sorry, I just can't believe I'm here. And that you're there."

"You and me both. Take a seat."

I sit in the matching armchair next to Ruby. The years have been kind. She looks exactly as I pictured her. She's still slim. Time sprinkled tiny moles across her sharp facial features. She's gotten more beautiful with age. Her blue eyes are paler, most likely from cataracts.

"I just got back from the church service. It was really beautiful tonight, with the singing and lights and community. Throughout the entire service, I was hoping I would see you there."

"Really? What made you hope that?"

"Well, I heard you were back in town. I didn't believe it at first, but I knew it was true when everyone was talking about the famous artist in town."

"I tell you, this place is too small to exist in."

"Yeah, for folks who went off to do big things. For the rest of us, it's not so bad. It's nice to know neighbors and to go to your usual grocery store. See your friends at bingo night and at the post office."

"I guess it has its certain charms, but I sure don't miss it."

It doesn't surprise me that our conversation would be so easy. It always was. But it still feels different. Something is hanging in the air between us, something unsaid and unfinished. We're practically strangers. How does one even go about catching up for the lost time?

"Would you like some cocoa? I make it from scratch every year, my mama's recipe."

"I remember. I would love a cup, thank you."

Ruby gets up from her chair and grabs a cane I hadn't noticed. I was so caught up in the fact that Ruby was in front of me that I hadn't looked at her in her entirety. I wonder what the cane is for. Could it be something serious or does she just have bad knees?

"I haven't had someone visit me for Christmas in years." Ruby hands me the cup of cocoa.

"I heard."

"Who did you hear that from?"

"Amber at the front desk."

"Oh yeah, that sounds about right. Sweet girl, but she's the mouth of the South."

"Reminds me of someone I used to know," I say with a smirk.

"Who me?"

"Yes, you."

"I don't recall that."

"I'm sure you don't."

We sit in comfortable silence drinking our warm drinks, not knowing where to start with all the lingering questions between us.

"I have to tell you somethin', Ruby."

"This sounds serious. Hold on. Let me get my glasses." She adjusts brown, plastic frames and gives me her full attention.

"I didn't just come to town out of the blue."

"I figured. You were never the type to do things out of the blue. You always had a plan."

"I guess I do." I think about my awakening plan that led me to this very moment.

"So why did you come to town?"

It's either now or never, Juliet. Let it all go.

"I came to town to see you. Some months back, I was watching a film that brought back all the memories we shared. I thought I had forgotten them. I thought I had stored those memories somewhere in my brain to stay locked away until my final days. But there they were, flooding back as if it were yesterday. I had to find you, Ruby. I hated how everything ended."

The laughter and music from the holiday party contrast with our silence.

"I don't know what to say." Juliet twirls a loose piece of yarn hanging from her sweater.

"I think your silence says more than enough. I shouldn't have come. It was selfish, and I was only thinking about myself." I get up from my seat and head to the door.

"Juliet, wait! I'm glad you came. I'm silent because I'm surprised. And you can't just run away when things don't go according to your plan, especially when there's another person involved. Please take a seat."

I forgot how much Ruby knows me. She was never afraid to call me out.

"It's been a long time since we've seen each other. I would be lying to myself, and you, if I said my heart didn't skip a beat when I heard you were in town. It almost jumped out of my chest when Amber told me the name of my visitor. My life has been full of failed relationships. Ours was the most taboo, but it was the steadiest relationship I ever had. I thought about you throughout the years, more than you know."

"I'm sorry for that day in the hotel room. I was a coward."

Ruby lifts her hand to stop me from going on. "That's the past. And I've spent many years healing from the past. I don't want to rehash it."

"Okay, understood."

"So you came back to just see me?"

"No, it's a long shot, but I came back to see if we can finally be together."

Ruby stares at me. I don't know what's going through her mind. It's making me more and more antsy with each silent passing second.

"We can't be together, Juliet."

I freeze. "Well, why not? I know there are a lot of years between us, but like you said, we don't have to focus on the past. We can start fresh and keep growing old and wrinkly together like you always wanted us to do."

"That's not why we can't be together. We can't be together because I'm dying, Juliet. I only have a couple of months left in me. And that's if I'm lucky."

It's as if the wind has been knocked out of me. Dying. I've been searching for her for months. Meanwhile, she only has roughly two months to live.

"How long have you known?"

"For some time now. I've done all the chemo rounds a few times, but enough is enough. I'm not afraid of dying that much to do another one."

Tears are falling uncontrollably down my face. "I wish I had looked for you sooner."

"If you had, what would we have done that we can't do now?"

"For starters, we would get you out of here and find a little place together. Somewhere warm, perhaps by some water like the ocean or the sea."

Ruby smiles. "Go on."

"We would spend our days cooking, dancing, throwing small parties with all our friends in the area. And we would go to sleep together, and wake up next to one another, and we would lay there in each other's arms, knowing that we have nowhere to be and nothing to do except be in that bed with each other."

"That does sound nice." Ruby slaps her hand on her thigh. "It's settled. That's what we're going to do. It'll be an early Christmas gift from you to me."

"Excuse me?"

"You didn't come all this way just to see me in this retirement community. You've had that vision for a long time. I've had that vision for a long time. You can't imagine how many times I've had a dream of us running off together and living the life we dreamt of as girls. If all we got is two months left, then that's what we're going to do. I don't have time to hold a grudge. I don't have time to waste. But I do have lots of money to get rid of, and you've always had an eye for beauty. You find the place, and I'll pay."

"I don't know if this is a good idea."

"It's a great idea. Besides, you wouldn't say no to a dying woman, would you?"

"You always did know how to get what you want."

"It's a gift. Now get looking and booking. We don't have all day."

It only takes us an hour or so to decide we're going to Mexico. I found a beautiful home by the ocean, and it won't be a long flight, given Ruby's condition. I called Theodore, and he brought my things over from the bed-and-breakfast.

"Everything is happening so fast." I'm booking the tickets and accommodation while Ruby packs.

"Are you kidding? All of this is fifty plus years in the making."

I laugh. "I guess you're right about that. Our flight leaves in the morning."

It doesn't take long for Ruby to finish packing. "I refuse to travel with a heavy load. I want to be light. Besides, I'm not gonna need any of this stuff soon anyway."

We leave her small apartment to join the holiday festivities in the community room. Ruby is just as popular as she was when we were growing up. Everyone wants to stop and talk to her, give her gifts, and meet her new guest.

"This is Juliet, my dearest friend and the love of my life," Ruby says with her arm wrapped around mine. I'm speechless. And by the wide eyes and gaping mouths of the residents, so are they.

Ruby only laughs. "I've been waiting a long time to say that!" She takes my hand in hers and squeezes. "Now, let's go dance and give these old folks something they can really stare at."

She leads me to the dance floor. It feels like I'm dreaming. Earlier today I was too afraid to come here and see Ruby. Now here I am at a party with her and preparing to fly to another country with her. We're preparing to spend the rest of her days together.

We dance until our feet ache. At first, everyone stares. Some even spit out, "They should be ashamed of themselves!" before leaving the party in disgust. "This is a holiday celebration. They should've kept their relationship private instead of parading it around in all of our faces!"

We're definitely parading, but we couldn't care less whose face it's in. No one blinks an eye at the man and woman couples dancing beside us. I suppose no one ever blinked an eye when I was with Roy. And when I went out with Elena we were always amongst people of all different ages. This isn't San Francisco in the sixties and seventies. This is the Bible-belt South, and we're meant to act accordingly. Ruby doesn't care one bit, and her courage is contagious. We've waited a long time to dance like this. Not knowing how long we have together is a lingering thought in my mind. If I care more about appeasing others than being fully with the person I love, time will fly by and I'll be left with regret.

***

We're standing in our pajamas on opposite sides of her queen-sized bed. "Does this feel like a dream to you?"

"Yes! I've been secretly pinching myself all evening."

"Do I feel like a stranger to you?"

Ruby shakes her head. "No, of course not. Do I to you?"

I shake my head. "No."

Ruby sits on the bed with her back against the headboard and pats the spot next to her.

"I know there's a lot of unspoken things between us. And I promise we can talk as much about our past as your heart desires once we get to Mexico. We haven't seen each other since we were in our thirties, but I can assure you, Juliet, that my feelings for you have not changed."

"What you want to say is stop overthinking, Juliet."

"Exactly."

"Fine, I hear you loud and clear."

We turn off the lamps on the nightstands and slide under the blanket. The hall outside the door is quiet. The only light in the room is coming from the window. I reach for Ruby's hand. Not long after, we fall asleep with our fingers intertwined.

Chapter Twenty-Three

MEXICO IS HOT AND beautiful, which is quite refreshing for my body, coming from the cold. We make it to Cabo San Lucas in one piece after our night of dancing. I sniff the fresh and salty ocean air as we walk toward our rental. My stomach flips with excitement at the thought of sinking my feet into the warm waters while the sun soaks into my bare skin. Our villa is right on the beach. And the ocean is our backyard. It's vast, breathtaking, and worth every penny. Colorful art draws the eye throughout the home, contrasting with the white furniture in the spacious rooms. The decor blends high-end modern furnishings with traditional textiles and pottery. It's an artist's dream. A welcome basket of wine and fruit sits on the counter.

"Oh yeah, I think I'm going to like Mexico," I say with a big smile. Ruby laughs as she takes in the house and finally the view from the large patio.

"Look at that view of the ocean. It's perfect."

"There are a lot of retirees in this town, so I'm sure it won't be hard to find a little community here."

"That's great. Although if I spent my time with just you, I would be perfectly content."

"Me too. Now you go take a shower and get some rest. Tonight we're going out on the town." I tease her with a shimmy of my hips.

"You always were the wild one."

"So I've been told. Now get!"

I can tell Ruby needs rest. I can also tell she's not going to let me know how her body is feeling. I've done this before, tending to a dying person...three times now. It's far from easy. I must take into consideration her mind, body, and spirit, as well as my own. The process can be an overwhelming shock to the nervous system.

I don't want to think about what's to come. I must live in what is. Right now she needs lots of fresh fruit and veggies, and of course some sweet chocolate treats. I grab an empty bag and head down to a market we passed on our way here.

Ruby sleeps for the majority of the day, while I pull out my traveling paint kit and walk to the beach. I'm spending Christmas Eve in Mexico with the one person I thought I would never see again.

I'm finishing the outline of my painting when my phone vibrates. "Hello."

"Mom?"

A slow smile spreads across my face as the familiar voice says the one word I've been missing for a week. "Toni, it's so nice to hear your voice."

"It's even better to hear yours. Happy Christmas Eve."

"Happy Christmas Eve to you too." I can hear the faint sound of sniffling through the phone. "Is everything all right?"

"No. I'm sorry for my reaction at your dinner. You didn't deserve that. I've always hated change, you know that. But it's the one thing I probably need the most in my life."

I give Toni the time and space she needs to open up fully, without interruption. If she's calling, there must be something weighing on her heart.

"I have to leave Steven."

I sit up straighter in my chair because I was not expecting those words to come out of her mouth. "Why?"

"Well for starters, he's been cheating on me for years. I stayed because I wanted this perfect image of what a family looks like. Not to mention he's just a complete narcissistic asshole. I've always wanted what you and Daddy had. And when you told all of us about Elena and Ruby, it shattered the image I'd created of you two. And the image of my husband and me. I was angry at you because you were brave enough to take control of your life, when I've given my control away so easily."

"You know your father and I weren't perfect, Toni. We were far from it. We had ups, downs, sideways, diagonals. You name it, we had it. But we did have a strong love that always brought us back together. I'm fortunate that we had that. But you're your own woman, and you have your own journey in this life. You have to do what's best for you. Don't do what you think I would do. Don't do it for your children. Do it for yourself."

"But it's not easy. He was the first person I ever loved." Toni's voice cracks. I wish I were there to cradle her in my arms.

"That doesn't mean he'll be the last. And if you need a place to go, you know my door's always open. You have a spare key.'"

"Thanks, Mom. I miss you. When are you coming home?"

"I miss you too, Toni. It may be a while. I'm in Mexico right now with Ruby."

"Wait, Mexico! You found her?"

"Yes, I did. We'll be here for a bit."

"I'm sure you're expecting a Toni lecture about how irresponsible it is that you went all the way to Mexico without informing your family. Honestly, Mom, I wish I were as brave as you."

"Don't be so hard on yourself. Give it time. You'll get there. You're my daughter after all."

We end the call with updates on the grandchildren. I've been texting with Destiny nonstop, giving her updates on Ruby and me, but it's nice to hear what everyone is up to. I walk back inside as the sun sets to find Ruby in the kitchen eating the papaya I cut up for her.

"This is just what I needed. Didn't realize how famished I was."

"How'd you sleep?"

"Like a newborn baby. That bed is heaven!"

"You sure you want to go out tonight? It was just a suggestion. I'm okay with staying in."

"Oh no, we're going out. We'll have plenty of lazy days together. It's Christmas Eve and I'm feeling festive!"

We walk through the bustling town filled with music, Christmas decorations, and the delicious aromas of street food.

"Looks like the people here know how to party," Ruby says.

We find a seat at a table on the beach. Couples are dancing to the Christmas music blasting from the speakers, while the kids are playing tag. All I can do is look at Ruby. A couple around our age walks over from a table nearby.

"Sorry to bother you two. Are you new here?" the woman asks.

"Just got in today," I say.

"How wonderful. Are you two on vacation or here to stay for a while?"

"We're here for a while." Ruby squeezes my hand.

They pull chairs up to our table. "Mind if we sit?" the man asks.

I motion with an upturned hand. "By all means."

"Sorry for being so forward. We just get excited when we see fellow expats our age. I'm Tracy. This is my boyfriend, Carl."

"Nice to meet you, Tracy and Carl. I'm Ruby and this is my partner, Juliet. You two been here long?"

"For about ten years now. We came here as widows. I met him on the second day I arrived."

"How romantic!"

"Oh it was. It's like the stars brought us together. How did you two meet?"

Ruby and I look at one another and smile. "We met when we were about six years old. Ruby's mother and my mother became friends and so did we."

"Wow, I just know there's a story there. You two are going to have to come over to our place for dinner. We'll have a party to welcome you to town so you can meet some of the other retirees in the community."

"That sounds wonderful!" Ruby says.

We talk with Carl and Tracy for the whole night. We even meet some of their friends. At one point, we find ourselves all dancing on the beach under the stars. Before we part ways, we make plans to go to their house for dinner in a couple of days.

I lay in bed wide awake, too energized to fall asleep. I still can't believe she's lying right beside me. I see every version of her whenever I look at her face. I see Ruby as a child, and the rebellious teenage Ruby, and all the Rubys after that. The clock hasn't stopped ticking in my head. I'm trying so hard to soak in as much of her as I can while I can.

"Aren't you going to go to sleep?" She turns her head to look at me.

"I thought you were asleep."

"Kind of hard to sleep when someone's staring at you."

"Some people think it's romantic."

"Those people are wrong."

I stare up at the ceiling, listening to our soft breaths mingle with the sound of the waves.

"Juliet?"

"Yeah."

"I'm sorry."

I turn to face her. "Sorry for what?"

"I'm sorry for showing up that day at your hotel in Ireland. I should've never put you in that position. You had a family, a husband and a daughter. I shouldn't have tried to make you choose between me and them."

I grab her hand. "It's in the past, right?"

"Yes, yes it is."

"Then let's leave it there."

After a few silent seconds, she turns to face me again. "We haven't kissed yet."

"Well it's only been two days since we've been reunited."

"So what? Are you trying to make it three?"

"Not exactly."

"I always pictured us embracing each other, if we were to ever reunite, and sealing it with a kiss."

"I did too. But it's been so long. I didn't want to push too far too soon."

She leans over and rests the palm of her hand on my cheek. "I want to be pushed. The further and sooner the better." Ruby leans in closer and brushes her lips against mine. They're still soft and full. We don't do more than kiss. It's a gentle moment that requires gentle actions. Being with Ruby doesn't make me yearn for passion and sex. We've had that many times. Being with Ruby makes me yearn for tender moments together. Time. That's all I want.

Chapter Twenty-Four

"MERRY CHRISTMAS, JULIET!"

"Merry Christmas, Ruby!" My voice is groggy and there's still sleep in the corner of my eyes, but the smell of warm maple syrup, cinnamon, and freshly cut tropical fruit helps to fully wake me as I sit up in bed. Ruby sets a stack of pancakes on my lap, and I lean over to give her a morning kiss. "Breakfast in bed, I haven't had this since Mother's Day when Toni was a girl. Everything looks delicious."

Ruby sits next to me with two forks in hand. "I hope it tastes as good as it looks. I had to go to three different tiendas and the mercado early this morning, just to find all the ingredients."

"You went alone? Why didn't you wake me? I could've gone with you." I'm picturing all the things that could've gone wrong with Ruby being out there on her own in her condition.

"Yes, I went alone. I wanted to do something special for you, and I couldn't do that if you were right beside me, now could I?"

I take a bite of the fluffy pancake. "I guess not. But next time can you at least let me know you're going out? You don't have to tell me where."

I can tell she wants to resist. There's nothing worse than having to check in with someone before you can live your life. Toni tries to have me do the same thing. I never listen, but she tries. This is different. I don't want to control Ruby. I wish I didn't have to know her whereabouts, but both Ruby and I know it's for the best.

"Okay." She quickly changes the subject. "Now, how are the pancakes?"

"Delicious. You'd better hurry and eat some or I may devour the entire stack."

"You eat as much as you like. I'm fine with the fruit."

I look out the open window at the morning sun and shimmering ocean.

"I also got you this." She pulls out a wrapped gift box covered in snowmen, with a green bow on top.

"You didn't have to get me anything."

"This is our first Christmas together in more than half a century. Of course I had to get you something. I *wanted* to get you something."

I slowly open the perfectly wrapped gift. Inside is a dark mahogany chest filled with small porcelain bowls, watercolor bricks, and brushes.

"Ruby, where did you find this? It's beautiful!"

"I've had it for over twenty years. I was in France on vacation, shopping of course, when I stumbled into this tiny antique shop. I don't know what made me stop. I had already been out shopping all day and was exhausted by that point. I walked in and found this nineteenth century watercolor set sitting in the corner. I immediately thought of you and how you always wanted to live and paint in France when you were younger."

"You bought it because of me?"

"I did. I had no idea what I was going to do with it. I considered looking you up and shipping it to you, but I could never bring myself to do it. I kept it on my dresser. Every time I looked at it, I thought of you and of all the beautiful moments we shared."

Teardrops fall onto the wooden box in my lap. She thought of me all those years in between just as much as I thought of her.

"Thank you, Ruby."

She lightly wipes away the tears from my face. "Now, what did you get me?" She's reminding me of how excited she used to get when we were girls exchanging handmade gifts for Christmas and birthdays.

"I didn't know we were getting gifts. Everything has been so last minute."

"Oh no, of course. That's okay, being with you is more than enough." I can tell she's trying to hide her disappointment as she picks at the fruit on the plate. Someone knocks on the front door.

"I'll get it." She's visibly relieved to have an excuse to leave the room.

"Hola, are you Señora Juliet?" the man at the door asks.

"No, I'm Ruby. Can I help you with something?"

"Feliz Navidad, Ruby! We're here to take you and Señora Juliet on your whale-watching tour."

Ruby turns to me with a huge smile on her face. "You didn't?"

"Of course I did. It's Christmas after all. I packed our bags last night, so we're ready to go."

It's the humpback whale's mating season here in Cabo San Lucas. Christmas decorations adorn the boat, where we're offered cocktails and champagne. Our feast is an assortment of fruit, cheese, wraps, crackers, and yummy ceviche. Our tour guides, Eduardo and Manuel, are in their early thirties, lively, and extremely funny. We pass through the famous Arch of Cabo San Lucas under a clear, cobalt-blue sky with barely a cloud in sight.

Every time we spot a humpback, her eyes light up. I could never understand where her fascination for whales came from. She's had it since we were little girls. We would be swimming in the lake on a hot summer day, while our mothers sat on the dock watching us. Ruby would dive underwater, pop back up, and blow water out of her mouth.

***

"That's disgusting, Ruby!" I wiped away some spit that found its way to my face.

"No, it's not. I'm a whale."

"You're a whale in a lake?"

"Yep, why not?"

"I think you need to be in the ocean to be a whale."

"Well, one day I'm gonna go to the ocean and see one."

"Yeah okay. I'd love to see that happen."

***

Here we are, six decades later, whale watching on the ocean.

"Aren't they just majestic?" Ruby's gaze is glued to the water.

"Yeah, they are. I've never been so close to a creature so big."

"Me neither. We humans think we're so grand and larger than life. But look at the ocean, the whales, the mountains. We're just tiny, little specs in comparison. We take ourselves so seriously. Everything we do seems so important, but eventually, it'll all come to an end and we'll turn into even smaller specs."

Ruby's expression grows distant. I'm not sure if she's looking at the whales or nothing at all. I reach for her hand and hold on until she turns to face me.

"Thank you, Juliet. This is the best gift I've ever received."

We watch the whales in silence, listening to the songs of brown pelicans and the ocean.

***

"We don't have to go to the dinner. You should rest. That's more important."

I pat a cool cloth against Ruby's forehead and cheeks. The past two days since Christmas have been the ultimate reminder that I'm not only here spending time with Ruby. I'm here spending time with a very ill and dying Ruby. I've been feeding her nourishing broth and smoothies, on and off, throughout the day. She's finally able to keep something down after two days of nothing sticking. I've been cleaning up vomit and tending to her every need. With each passing day, her bones become more pronounced. Her face seems sunken, and the whites of her eyes show a tinge of yellow. She looks at me with the biggest smile, as if doing so doesn't use up most of her energy.

"Don't be silly. They're throwing a dinner party for us. I've been messaging Tracy all afternoon. They're so excited, and so am I. I didn't come to Mexico to just stay in bed. If I wanted to do that, I would've stayed at the retirement community."

"But do you have the strength to go?"

"Juliet, we're going. That's final. Even if you have to push me there in a wheelchair, we will be sitting at that dinner table, all dressed up, meeting people from all over the world. People who are coming to meet us."

"Well that's exactly what we'll do then. I'll call around to see if I can find a wheelchair."

***

We're wearing our best evening attire, as I push Ruby to the dinner party. Tracy and Carl live in a luxurious villa surrounded by trees, with one of the best views of the ocean. Several people

are already inside, mingling around the dinner table. The
spread of fresh seafood, cheeses, wine, desserts, and fruit make
my mouth water.

"I cannot believe you two did all of this for us. The
decorations are beautiful."

"We love to throw parties. And we had such a great time the
other night that we wanted to make this special to welcome you
two," Tracy says.

"It's definitely special. Thank you both." I give Tracy a warm
smile. Everyone we meet is friendly. With each new person, I
become more and more comfortable with Ruby introducing me
as her partner. The vibes of the party are light and loose, a bit
eccentric, yet welcoming. We're among fellow artists and
travelers near our age. I suspect these folks may have taken the
road less traveled once or twice in their life. I don't feel judged.
I don't feel as if I have to prove myself or be someone I'm not.
The party has a similar feeling to when I went clubbing with
Destiny. I've been hungry for this feeling of freedom my entire
life.

By the early hours of the morning, we feel like we're a part of
the community here. We've been invited out by everyone we've
met. Although I enjoyed myself immensely, I can tell the night
has taken a toll on Ruby. She doesn't say anything, but her body
is speaking loud and clear. I help remove her party clothes
when we make it back to the house, and I run a warm bath.

"You don't have to do this, you know. I didn't want to run off
with you just so you can be my caretaker."

"Come on, Ruby, you know me well enough to know I am
perfectly happy taking care of you for as long as you need me
to."

"Yeah, I know. You were always so good at taking care of
everyone. I just wish I could return the favor."

I help her to fully undress. She stands in front of me. Bare.
Aged. She's just as beautiful as when she stood in front of me at
sixteen. Before I can think, my hand moves up to gently trace
the curve of her neck and the sharp line of her collarbone. My
fingers slide down and up the soft slope of her arm, until my
palm rests in the middle of her chest. I close my eyes and feel
the thump of her heart flowing through my hand. Oh, how I
wish I could freeze this moment. Her heart is beating. Her flesh

is soft and warm, and her eyes are closed with the promise of soon reopening.

"Will you join me, Juliet?"

I nod, slowly peeling off my layers and allowing for Ruby's eyes to take me in. She grabs my hand and walks me to the bath. We submerge our bodies in the warm water, and I surrender to the now. Anything that requires concern will have to wait until tomorrow.

Chapter Twenty-Five

I FIND IT IRONIC how I spent so much of my time these past few months focused on living only to be surrounded by death. When I first cared for my dying mother, I thought I could do it all. I thought by doing everything I could to provide her with comfort, I would somehow be able to alleviate her pain and suffering. In the end, I was wrong. I knew there was nothing I could do to ease my father's discomfort. I watched in horror each day as the inevitable approached. With Roy, I was a complete shell of myself. *I* was the one suffering. *I* was the one who needed comfort. My wonderful husband, who I know was deeply in pain, attempted to mask his pain as much as possible to comfort me. This time with Ruby is different. I understand what is to come. I also understand that showing up for Ruby, being fully present and making sure she knows I'm here and she's not alone is enough. Ruby's journey is already set in stone. I cannot save her. I cannot prolong her life. But I can be here. And I can be okay with the fact that my presence is enough.

I'm also human, and I hate watching Ruby's body grow thinner with each passing day. I hate cleaning up her vomit. Or waking up in the middle of the night to her moans as she clenches her body in pain. There's never been a time in my life when I've felt as helpless as when I'm sitting next to someone who's dying. Is this how a man feels as they watch a woman give birth? Helpless, fearful, in awe of life itself. I savor the moments when Ruby's body is at peace. We read together and share stories of the in-between years of our lives. We drink tea out on the patio or at the beach, where we make a game of who can spot a whale first. Time is moving quickly, I'm sitting out on the patio, drinking a mango smoothie, when my phone rings. I expect it to be Destiny or Toni. When I see Elena's name on the screen, I sit up straighter in my lounge chair and my heart quickens. "Hello."

"Juliet."

"Elena, I wasn't expecting your call."

"I know. You were just on my mind, so I figured I'd give you a call."

"Well, I'm glad you did. What are you up to?"

"I just finished a table set for a client. Now I'm sitting in the café drinking coffee."

"You're at our café?"

"The one and only."

"God, I miss their chai tea."

"It'll be here whenever you get back. If you come back." The phone is silent for a moment before she clears her throat. "Did you find her?"

"Yes."

"Good. I'm happy for you. I don't want to keep you long, but whenever you're back in town, I'd love to see you...and meet Ruby."

Tears form quickly in the bottoms of my eyelids, and there's a golf ball stuck in my throat. I manage to say, "Okay. That'll be nice. Take care, Elena."

"You too, Juliet."

The picturesque view of the ocean blurs as tears flow uncontrollably down my face.

"Juliet?"

Ruby's soft voice makes me jump. I hurry to help her take a seat next to me while trying and failing to hide my tear-stained face.

"Who's Elena?"

I wipe my face. "She's a good friend."

Ruby looks at me with her head tilted slightly to the side. "Juliet, I know when you're not telling me everything. You know that."

I do, and I know she's not going to leave it alone until I tell her the whole truth. "She's a woman I'd been seeing for some months before I found you."

"You were dating her?"

"Yes."

"And she knows about me?"

"Yes."

"And she still called to check on you?"

"Yeah. She says she wants to meet you one day."

Ruby sits back in the lounge chair and folds her hand on her stomach. She's looking up at the sky. "How interesting. Why didn't you tell me about her?"

"I didn't think I'd hear from her again. So I didn't see the point."

"I see. But you cared for this woman?"

"We cared for each other, yes."

"Okay."

"Okay?"

"Okay. Now on to more pressing matters. What's for dinner?"

We go about the rest of our day following our normal routine. Ruby has just enough energy to go out to a small restaurant for dinner. We stay for a while, listening to a live band. Ruby makes it easy for people to fall in love with her, always has. Our new friends flock to our table, and she makes everyone feel important. She listens without needing to always speak. She tells stories that make you feel as if you're there. Her light has always been bright, and by the time you're done talking with her, your light is just as bright. I've always admired the way she moves through this world. No one is a guest, and everywhere is home.

***

Something tells me to go to the bathroom at four in the morning. I'm stumbling out of bed and groggy, but I go. Ruby is collapsed on the floor next to the bathtub.

"Ruby!"

I race over to her and check her pulse. She's still breathing, but she's unconscious. I use all my strength to pull her out of the bathroom and somehow into the bed. It's a slow process, but we eventually get there. I hurry to wet a cloth to dab around her face. After a minute or so, she stirs.

"What happened?" She can barely make out her words. I help her take a sip of water.

"I think you fainted in the bathroom."

"How did I get in the bed?"

"I brought you in here."

She tries to nod, but her head barely moves. Her hand reaches for me, and I gently take her hand in mine. I take her other hand and try to thaw the ice.

"Lay with me Juliet."

I lie next to her in the early morning hours. Her breathing is so faint I have to strain my ears to hear it.

"I love you, Juliet."

"I love you too, Ruby."

"I've always loved you. Since I first saw you with your mom, wearing that big green bow in your hair. I begged my mom to go and talk to yours because I wanted to be your friend." Ruby smiles. "You think I'll see her again?" she asks.

"Your mom?"

She nods.

"I think so."

"I hope I do. I've missed her for a long time." Her eyes become glossy. "I think it'll be soon, Juliet. Sooner than we thought."

I bring her hand up to my lips as tears run from my eyes. "I never thought we would have this long, but we did it."

"Did what?" she asks softly.

"We grew old and wrinkly together. At least for a short while."

She turns her head to look at me. "We did, didn't we?"

"Are you afraid?"

"Of what?"

"Dying."

A slow smile spreads across her face. Her eyes shimmer like moonlight on the ocean. "Not anymore."

Chapter Twenty-Six

I REMEMBER RUBY SAYING how she always wanted her ashes spread over the ocean. The water is up to my knees. The skirt of my white dress flows with the waves. This is the last time I'll hold Ruby. The water is so clear I can see fish circling my feet and underwater plants swaying to and fro. I scatter her ashes without saying anything. Everything that needed to be said between us has already been said. As I walk toward shore, I hear water shoot out from the blowhole of a whale somewhere in the distance. Turning around, I smile. "I love you too, Ruby."

I fly out of Mexico and arrive back home before sunset. It's strange being back. If it weren't for the sadness, I would believe that this last month or so has all been a dream. I feel like a ghost haunting my own house. I'm here, but I'm not here. I wander aimlessly from room to room with tears in my eyes. My body is heavy, like I'm carrying two sacks of potatoes on each shoulder. My appetite is nonexistent, and all I want to do is sleep. Which is exactly what I do, on and off, for three days straight. I turn off my phone and allow my body to release everything I've been holding onto from the moment Ruby took her last breath to the moment I walked back into this house. I scream. I cry. I laugh, thinking of all our memories together, until my belly aches. Eventually, I sit in silence, feeling nothing. Even our emotions need time to rest.

On day four, the sun shines through the window. I notice I'm not as sad as I have been. I don't feel as heavy, but my motions are still slow. I take a shower, then make a pot of tea and start a fire. Despite the sun, there's still inches of snow outside. Surprisingly, the winter landscape brings a tiny smile to my face. I drink my tea at the kitchen table and sift through the mail Destiny and Toni brought in while I was away. My eyes zoom in on a large manilla envelope addressed to me from Ruby. With shaking hands I open the letter.

Dear Juliet,

You're probably wondering when I had the time to write this letter and mail it. Let's just say I know how to make connections quickly to get things done. There's not much left to be said between us. As I write this, I don't know how long I have left, but I couldn't have asked for a better person to spend the rest of my days with. You will always be the love of my life, Juliet. And because of this, I leave everything to you.

Juliet, your heart is too big, and your love is too sacred to spend the rest of your years alone, grieving over the loves you have lost. I don't know who Elena is, but something tells me she's a keeper. And before you can even think it, no, being with Elena doesn't mean you're replacing me. So don't even think it! I don't want to make this letter long. I just want to remind you that you have been down this road before. You've grieved. And although aging doesn't make grief hurt any less, it can help us learn how to grieve better. Grieve better than the last time, Juliet. Don't allow so much time to go by before you continue to keep living. Time is the most precious gift we receive from birth. So do me one last favor and keep living your life fully with the precious time you have.

Love,
Ruby

Two days later, after reading the letter for the hundredth time, I turn my phone on and call Elena. My fingers are trembling. The pounding of my heart echoes off the kitchen walls.

"Juliet?"

The voice on the other end is reassuring, giving me the confidence to go through with this.

"Hi, Elena."

"It's nice to hear from you."

I remind myself to keep talking. This is what Ruby would want. "I'm back in town. You wanna grab a coffee and chai? At our usual spot?"

I wait for her to respond, but the other line is completely quiet. I pull the phone away to confirm I didn't accidentally hang up. "Elena, you there?"

"I'm here, sorry. I was thinking about the last time we saw each other at the museum."

"Oh, right." I recall a goodbye I both regret and don't regret. If I had stayed, I would have missed the last moments of Ruby's life.

"There was a painting…"

"The Picasso?"

"Yeah, that one. I thought about that painting so many times after that day. I thought I would never see you again. And I was so sad that a painting filled with so much pain and sadness would be the last image I would have of our time together. But now, here you are calling to see if we can go to the café."

I begin to worry that calling her was a mistake. Seconds tick slowly away. I hold my breath, waiting for her to turn down my invitation.

"I'll meet you there in an hour," she says and hangs up the phone.

And just like that, hope returns.

***

My knee doesn't stay still underneath the table. I'm more nervous than I was on our first date. I'm waiting for Elena at my favorite spot by the window. Nerves override logic. Is this a big mistake? I glance around in search of the door to the kitchen. There must be a back door, if I need to sneak out without her seeing me.

As I prepare to slide out of the chair, I see Elena before she sees me. I don't have an impulse to run, at least not in the opposite direction. My stomach flutters and my bouncing knee settles. By the time Elena makes it to the table, my lips are spread in a wide smile. The sadness still lingers, but the joy of seeing Elena is present as well. Perhaps Ruby was right. Maybe I can grieve better than the last time.

"I must say, Juliet, you're a sight for sore eyes." Elena wraps me in a hug so tight and warm I linger a bit, then quickly pull away. It doesn't feel right. Not yet.

"Where's Ruby? I was expecting her to join us."

Hearing her mention Ruby, as if she's still here, sends unexpected tears down my face. Elena's hand on my shoulder is comforting.

"What happened?"

I motion for her to sit across from me. "Please sit."

She hands me a blue handkerchief out of her coat pocket. The customers sitting at the table next to us depart. It's just me and Elena in our intimate corner by the window.

"Thank you." I stare at the small white daisies embroidered around the edges of the handkerchief.

"I haven't seen one of these in ages."

"It was my mother's. I always keep it on me. She embroidered anything she could get her hands on."

"It's beautiful."

It must've taken hours to create something so delicate, so precise. When did I last give myself time to create something as beautiful as this? My fingers aimlessly trace the white thread forming the petals and the tear stain in the middle of the blue, cotton square.

"Is everything okay, Juliet? You don't look like your normal self."

I chuckle, wondering how my normal self looks to her. We all hold images of people like photographs in our mind. We assume those images will remain frozen, the same as they were the last time we saw them. I know I do, more than I care to admit.

"Yes. Everything's fine."

"Let me order the drinks."

I watch Elena from afar. She smiles at the barista, places the drink order, and returns.

"Now, tell me what happened."

"It's Ruby." I fidget with the corner of the handkerchief, allowing my mind to briefly focus on a present object instead of the bowling ball sitting in my chest.

"She passed away last week."

Even though Elena didn't ask to hear the whole story, I need to tell it. I need to recount these past weeks to remind myself it happened. It wasn't a dream. When I finish, she sits quietly. She's good at that, taking in what I say before responding.

Elena stands and takes my hand to help me up. She wraps her arms around me, her chin buried in my shoulder. Neither of us speaks. My body surrenders under her embrace, and I'm in no rush to pull away. This time, it feels right.

***

Elena and I don't jump back into how our relationship once was, meaning we're not sleeping together all the time. I may be trying to grieve better, but I *am* still grieving.

Time is fleeting as you age, but I'm happy going slow in this new chapter of our relationship. Our moments feel organic, and our relationship requires nurturing.

We spend a lot of time together. I call her whenever I need to vent or cry. We talk about the horrible reality dating show on Netflix that has become our guilty pleasure. We visit each other's homes. I remember where she keeps her favorite mug, and she remembers my favorite brand of tea and how I like honey instead of sugar. When I grocery shop, I pick up little things she likes, usually sweets for when she has the munchies. Ginger snaps and strawberry ice cream are favorites.

We go shopping for seeds and plants for our gardens. At least once a week, we go to the movies. It turns out she loves foreign indie films just as much as I do. Dancing is one of our favorite pastimes. Sometimes we go out, but most of the time we dance at home. Wherever we go, we move through spaces unabashedly together.

Each day is a new surprise. There is nothing planned or certain. We both are wise enough to not worry about empty calendars and living with a fear of missing out on something. We've both lived full, beautiful lives.

She doesn't push. I don't ask for more than I can handle. Ours is a partnership without expectation, one I am enjoying quite a bit.

Chapter Twenty-Seven

MY MIND, BODY, AND spirit needed to hibernate after Mexico. I was done running away from my emotions. Now I need a fresh start. Spring is waking from a long slumber. The birds are slowly returning to the trees. Each day, I notice stems of unknown plants burst through the soil in my dried-up garden. The snow is nearly gone, and children in the neighborhood chase after one another without a care in the world. I'm looking forward to the change of the season. It's the time of year for planting seeds and dreams, and patiently watching them grow. It's the time to lean forward into life once more, while keeping in mind all we've learned during the winter months.

I walk around my home, taking in memories of every corner and every crack. I no longer feel attached to any of it. It's time for a change. It's time to sell my house and start anew, perhaps far away in a distant land.

I've always believed I lived a rather simple life. Sure, I'm known for my paintings. Sure, I've seen the world and acquired many awards throughout my years, but it's not as if I've trekked through the Himalayas or gone scuba diving in Zanzibar. Most of my travels were work-related, never for pleasure. My life has been uniquely mine, but not necessarily special. I wake up in the morning and breathe. I eat breakfast and dinner. I go on walks and watch movies I've seen hundreds of times. I take naps and sing off-key to my favorite songs. Sometimes I laugh. Sometimes I cry. Sometimes I do both at the same time. My story is my story, but I wouldn't say that my story deserves praise. It will end like everyone else's. I will die, as will we all. But I can finally look at my simple little life and smile. What a life I have lived. What a life I am living. I do not need to run from grief. I couldn't even if I tried. I don't need to run from myself. I can't hide from those dark, silent moments. I can't always try to live in the light. Relationships will not save me from the fate I share with every living being. Neither will all the pleasures that come with life. But what I've learned since standing in front of that mirror on my birthday is that it's okay to surrender to all that life has to offer, both the ups and the downs. Surrender to the now. Surrender to what is. The more I did this on my journey, the more I allowed for every strand of the person I thought I was to unravel.

I walk over to open my bedroom window and let the cool, brisk air come through. Taking off my pajama top and bottom and throwing them on my unmade bed is an act of devotional love. I return to stand in front of the mirror that started it all. This time I no longer see the stretch marks on my thighs and stomach or the wrinkles on my hands, as being something to hide. I embrace my coily grey hair and wide hips, my brown skin and hanging breasts. I'm no longer just a body. I'm a body and spirit and so much more. I'm beyond beautiful. I'm ancient, young, holy, made up of every living being I see and even those that I don't. When I look in the mirror, I finally see God. I don't have to touch myself to know I'm here. And I no longer need the mirror to tell me I deserve to be here.

"You've come a long way, Peach."

Roy lies in the bed behind me. I walk over to him and cuddle up next to his side.

"Yeah I have, haven't I?"

"It seems like just yesterday you were standin' in that mirror having some sort of crisis."

"Life's funny like that. It's as if it happens in a blink of an eye."

"Don't I know it. Ya know, you haven't been calling on me as much, Peach. And it ain't like I'm not gonna miss your company, but I'm happy you're becoming happy with yourself and with those that you love."

"Me too, Roy."

"I'll see you around."

"You know where to find me."

It doesn't take long for my house to sell. Apparently, I live in an ideal area for young families. I thought I would feel a hint of sadness packing away my house into boxes and selling most of my items. But all I feel is a joyful freedom ready to burst from inside of me. The house is almost empty. Most of my belongings can now fit inside three suitcases and a few spare boxes. Just as I'm packing away my fine china, someone knocks on the front door. I've been so wrapped up in packing, I completely forgot I called for Toni to stop by.

"Hey, Mom."

I wrap my arms around Toni without saying a word. The exhaustion is written clearly across my daughter's face. I pull her inside and shut the door behind us.

"I can't believe you sold the house. And without talking to me about it first."

"Toni we've been over this. It was my house to sell, not yours."

"But this is my childhood home."

"And it always will be. But you're an adult, and you have your own house. You don't need this one too."

"Is there something equivalent to a midlife crisis for those over the midlife point?"

"Yes, but it's not a crisis. It's called being old and doing whatever the hell we please. Now come with me." I grab her hand and lead her toward my bedroom.

"Mom, why are you taking me to your room? And why was it so important for me to come over right away? I have a lot on my mind with this whole divorce thing."

"Because I have something for you." I lift the mirror off the ground and hand it to Toni.

"You're giving me a mirror?"

"It's not just any mirror. This mirror can change your life if you allow it to. All you have to do is set it up in your room and look at it. I prefer to look at myself naked, but that's just me."

"First off, that's too much information. And second, I don't know if a mirror is going to change anything."

"Toni, do you trust me?"

"Of course."

"Then for once, listen to your mother. I know a thing or two."

Toni reluctantly grabs the mirror and slumps down onto my bed. I flutter around the house like a hummingbird, packing last minute things away as I go.

"You know, Mom, I know I was hard on you for wanting to live your life the way you wanted to live it. I couldn't see the point then, but now I see it. You look like the one thing I'm trying to figure out how to have in my life right now. You're at peace."

I walk over to sit next to Toni, who no longer looks like the confident, put-together woman she's become. I see the little girl I would rock back to sleep after a bad dream. I brush away Toni's tears and give her hand a gentle squeeze.

"I feel at peace. But let me tell you something, little girl."—I lift Toni's chin so our eyes can meet—"If I can find peace, so can you. You're gonna get through this. You're far stronger, smarter, and more courageous than I ever was. Just take it day by day, and you'll see."

Toni leaves with the mirror that started it all. Hopefully, it'll help begin her journey of exploration and healing. Lili pulls up behind Toni and steps out of her car with her new Yorkshire terrier, Princess, in her arms.

"You know if you would've told me you would end up selling your house and moving abroad, I wouldn't have been so encouraging with that damn plan of yours."

"I'm going to miss you too, Lili." I hug her tightly as she quickly swipes away an escaped tear from her cheek.

"Maybe I should do something daring like you. Me and Princess here aren't getting any younger."

I grab her free hand. "Well in two months you'll get a taste of a daring adventure when we're on our girl's trip in Morrocco, dancing and drinking champagne under the stars."

Lili smiles and gives me another hug.

"I can't wait. Now you said something about a box of glassware, because if I stay out here any longer, I will be a blubbering mess."

"It's in the kitchen."

I wave goodbye to Lili and her dog, as Destiny and Kat pull into the driveway.

"And the goodbyes continue," I murmur.

Destiny hops out first.

"I can't believe you're leaving, Grandma!"

I embrace Destiny in a tight hug.

"You're always welcome to come and visit me, no matter where I am in the world. You and Kat both." Kat hurries onto the porch and joins in on the hug.

"I'm sure going to miss you, Ms. Juliet. You are sincerely my idol. But don't tell my Tía Elena. She thinks it's her."

"It'll be our little secret. Now there's a box for you girls in there filled with vintage clothes and knickknacks I think you two will love."

Before Destiny walks inside to see what's in the box I grab her hand.

"Thank you, Destiny, for everything."

Destiny wraps her arms around me once more.

"I'm so proud of you, Grandma. I love you."

"I love you too."

The girls grab the box, say their goodbyes, and drive off.

Back inside, I walk over to the kitchen window to look at the birds chirping nonstop on a branch directly in front of me.

"I know your secret," I say to them through the glass.

Non-humans never hold onto who they ought to be. They are who they are. They love who they love. They are born and they will die and continue into the next lifetime, and they will not ask why they are here. They will not say. Why me? Why was I given wings instead of arms? Why am I able to fly instead of swim? Why do I deserve to exist? I truly believe they have all the answers to the questions they will never ask. They have wings because they do. They fly because they can. And they are here because they are. I'm now content with the answer to the question hidden within my bones. I am here because I am. I have loved because I am love. I will die when I die. And I am alive because I am meant to be.

A knock comes from the front door. Elena stands behind the oak door looking radiant as always with two long, white braids hanging beneath a wide-brimmed hat. "Are you ready for Thailand?"

"Just about. Will these boxes fit in your truck?"

"Definitely, and you can store whatever you need in my workshop."

"Great. Thailand here we come!"

I hop into Elena's truck, suddenly giddy for our upcoming travels. As we drive away, every version of the Roy I once knew, from young to old, is waving from the front yard. "I'll miss you, Peach."

"I'll miss you too, Roy. I love you always!"

"Until we meet again, but not too soon I hope."

I smile. "No, not too soon."

I take Elena's free hand in mine as we drive. Our palms and fingers melt into one another's, as the wind brushes against my skin. After a lifetime of searching, I know what it means to live. There will be days when I will forget that I know. My humanness will convince me I don't know. But at this moment, as I stare out at the world with eyes that have been gazing for seventy-five years, I know. I don't need anything outside of myself to tell me who I am. I remember *exactly* who I am and why I'm here, in my body, alive. I understand now, birds, this is why you wake up in the morning with a song bursting from your chest. This is your secret. You're free. And so am I.

THE END.

About the Author

Rashah Solun is a writer from Atlanta, Georgia, whose stories explore the sacred and the forgotten, the seen and unseen. A graduate of Spelman College with a B.A. in Comparative Women's Studies, she weaves her love for quiet truths into her work. When she's not chasing after her spirited toddler, Rashah can be found savoring family moments, writing poetry, or lost in a good book with a warm cup of chai tea. Her life is a dance between the everyday and the liminal, where words become bridges to worlds both tender and profound.

Note to Readers

Thank you for reading a book from Launch Point Press. We have made every effort to edit this book. However, typos do slip in. If you find an error in the text, please email publisher@launchpointpress.com so the issue can be corrected.

We appreciate you as a reader and want to ensure you enjoy the reading process. We would like you to consider posting a review on your preferred media sites and/or your blog or website.

For more information on upcoming releases, author interviews, contests, giveaways and more, please sign up for our newsletter and visit us as at Launch Point Press: www.launchpointpress.com and "Like" us on Facebook: Launch Point Press.

Bright Blessings